ELEVATION

OF

MANA

✦ BOOK 3 ✦

ELEVATION

OF

MANA

✦ BOOK 3 ✦

WANDERING AGENT

Podium

Cover design by Yanhong Lu

ISBN: 978-1-0394-6655-5

Published in 2025 by Podium Publishing
www.podiumentertainment.com

Podium

ELEVATION OF MANA

OF

MANA

✧ BOOK 3 ✧

CHAPTER 1

JOURNEY OF A THOUSAND MILES

I was looking at the morning light, joined by those who were coming on the trek with me. Those that were staying behind stood away, and we checked our packs one final time. Auntie Atie, Ida, and Ian, who I was refusing to call my uncle, were all offering last bits of advice, particularly to the young Chien. While I'd not been looking, it appeared my aunt had apparently decided that she liked him, though in a way that reminded me of her treatment of me when I was younger.

Then there was the third wheel, so to speak, who stood nearby, her own leather pack tied tightly.

"You know, you don't have to come with us," I said to her.

"I am coming regardless, at least as far as that village. There are things that must be done, and I will be doing them." Her tone brooked no argument.

Jina had apparently decided that the pool needed to be either sealed or at least watched, and there was nobody more qualified than her to do it. She'd therefore declared that as we left she would be escorting us to whatever remained of Elayatol and taking care of the issue herself.

I found that I couldn't really argue against it. Cino's actions had proven that it was too dangerous to leave alone, even if he'd been considered mad by most of the current crop of elders. Was Jina the best person to do it? I honestly didn't know, but while she could be a grouch with a mean streak a mile long, she didn't seem to take it out on innocent bystanders. There was also a feeling that she was giving off, like she hurt and wanted to do something about it.

There wasn't much fanfare as we made our way to the gate and out into the surrounding lands. Some of the guards knew what was going on, and a few even nodded to me as we passed them, but the majority of the populace didn't. Even those acquainted with me were a little standoffish. The battle hadn't been so long ago, and the surrounding land was still scarred and poisoned from what I'd done. Given our outstanding memories, they were unlikely to change their opinions anytime soon.

We trudged westward toward the mountains. Those peaks helped us navigate borders, the large stone giants far less wooded than the thick forests, and faster to walk along, even if crossing them was a pain.

"Planning your way out?" Jina asked as we ate dinner, seeing that I'd drawn some squares on the ground.

"Yes, as much as I can. Any thoughts? I'm sure you've been to one of these places." I waved to the rough outline.

"I haven't actually, but I'll make one. Start with the north first, then work your way around. I know grandfather had a good relationship—or as much as he could have—with the old ruler of the northern wood. He's most likely to be friendly. I'd also avoid the inner lands if I were you. Cino's people are going to be in turmoil right now, and showing up won't be helpful."

That made as much sense as any other advice I'd heard. There were no maps of our lands as such, but rather the ideas of territories, and the people who lived near the edges all knew where those borders were. This made navigation difficult, if only because I had to try and find places that I had only verbal descriptions of. At least border disputes were rare, with wars like the one we'd just been in exceptionally so.

What I'd learned from the elders of Atal and some of those who traveled a bit wasn't all that helpful. Most of my people were fairly well dug in, not liking to go to and fro, and those who did often didn't end up going into the territories of other ancients. Even messages between them were sparse, meaning that some of my information could be painfully outdated.

Generally, though, our lands covered most of the eastern seaboard, a thick rainforest of dense growth up and along much of the coast. Going north from there, the climate cooled a bit and was more prone to floods. The northern wood was, if descriptions were to be believed, something more akin to a temperate zone, with less undergrowth and far larger trees. If anyone could really be considered a trading partner with the former city of Atal, it was the villages here.

If one went west through the northern wood, then they'd eventually find the coastline. That coast was dominated by a massive plateau. Again, information was sparse, but it seemed that other than a small green belt along the side, this geological feature dominated. One thing that everyone agreed on was that this region was bitterly cold, the altitude and winds causing the top of that plateau to freeze.

These three formed around the lands of the now deceased Cino. While the ancient that I'd killed possessed the most land—something else everyone agreed on—it was also viewed as some of the poorest. From what I understood, it was a large bowl of poor grassland, with few trees and fewer edible plants.

Below this, and sharing a border with both the lands of Atal and the west, were two known fiefdoms, both understood to be grassy and well off. There was also more to the south of them, but that was where reports really broke down, with conflicting answers to how many and what the rulers controlled.

It was my job to go to these various areas, find the ancients who ruled them, and inform those old monsters of the deaths of Atal and Cino. This was a tradition, a message sent to tell them that those who came to rule those lands were gone now.

"Do you think any of them will try to take Cino's or Atal's lands now that they're gone?" I asked Jina.

"If there is another close to becoming a proper ancient they might, if we're lucky," she answered, something which surprised me.

"If we're lucky?" I asked.

"Cino was a bastard, and we were at war, but if another his age decided to come and insert himself into the city, people would breathe easier." At my look she shook her head. "Yes, even me, so long as they ruled fairly. There are threats far worse than you've ever seen in this world, child. Threats best taken care of by the old. A good, ruling ancient can handle things even I cannot."

"But there are few," I added.

"Yes, few. As we get older, we fight others our age more. Many also end up fighting powerful monsters, and some fall before they are fully ancients. Their first few white hairs lead too many to believe they can handle anything. It is the cautious, lucky, and powerful who tend to survive the longest."

Those words caused me to sit and think until Chien came to tell me that dinner was done. I wondered if we could improve those numbers one day. It would be hard, of course, but perhaps we could have at least a few dozen ancients around to protect our people. That would certainly make our population safer.

CHAPTER 2

REMNANTS OF HOME

I stood at the edge, on the precipice, of a place I hadn't thought to see again so soon. It brought me no joy to come home, no pleasure seeing the place where I'd first entered this world. The valley sprawled out below me, but the village was unseen due to the high trees and vines.

The trip here had been easy enough. With the last of the Wester forces in full flight back to their homeland or being hunted like the dogs they were, there were few impediments. Of course, there were few places to stop as well, with most of the villages in this tract of land being destroyed, little left but ruins, if even those could be found. I wondered if there would be some kind of population boom, or if they'd move out of the city. A lot of older elves didn't like being kept under the heel of their elders and could probably be convinced to establish new villages. I'd even seen that one fighting over resources. If both of those factions had survived, I couldn't imagine that one or the other wouldn't just leave now, taking one of the large sections of now vacant territory.

Those thoughts managed to occupy my thoughts as we walked down the paths that two of us knew like the back of our hands. Isha was beside me, silent, for she'd been here when Cino arrived. The other two members of our party were behind us, keeping their eyes peeled.

As the village came into view, I knew there was nothing here for us. I'd hoped that someone had survived, that some others had made it out, but what I saw told me that was impossible. There'd been a part of me that had hoped one of the boys I'd grown up with was hiding somewhere, that Ninden would pop out of some bush with little Olond in tow, having managed to find a hole to crawl into while everything had been destroyed.

The houses left standing were overgrown. The forest was always making its inroads, after all, so this might have been ignored if someone wanted to remain unseen. The bodies, however, wouldn't have been. There weren't many, the time having elapsed since they'd destroyed this place. There wasn't a lot left, a few bones here and there. A skull sitting near the fire pit that we'd all gathered around so many times. None of our people would have left those had they known, had they come back home even after the Westers had left.

Isha sat down by the fire pit and began to weep, Jina comforting her as best she could.

"Anything I can do, boss?" Chien asked, seeming unsure of what he should be doing.

"Help me gather the bodies, if you can. Keep them together and mark where they came from. No real hope of knowing who was who, but it's something."

I spent a moment or two with the woman I loved, letting her cry onto my shoulder before I kissed her head and got to work. Everyone dealt with grief differently, myself included, and I knew what would help. I would work, something physical, something hard and sweat inducing. That would be better than crying, better than letting myself sink into despair. Thinking didn't appeal to me at the moment; nor did collapsing. That would only make me feel helpless.

My first home on this world was falling apart. It had been ransacked, ripped apart, and scattered. That stung, but it was clear why. There had been copper here. My father had worked it, known how it was made, and had some. They'd wanted that when they came through, to get it and use it. With Cala's hatred toward me, I didn't delude myself that either of my parents were alive. They'd known where I was and could have come as easily as Isha and Atie had. That told me I'd never see them alive again.

I thought I'd made my peace with the grief of losing my parents, but apparently not, for my heart ached as I moved through the remnants of my old home, looking for anything salvageable. There wasn't much, but I did manage to find an old digging stick. Not something anyone really liked, but something of use. There wasn't a scrap of metal left. Not a copper bead, not a tool; all of it thoroughly raided. I found one of the more isolated spots in the ruined village and began to dig. The graves didn't need to be too deep, but it didn't feel right leaving any bones that were left to the weather and any animals that might wander in after we left. No, they would have a burial. Perhaps not the proper one they'd have liked, but it was something.

It helped that this action was mindless. I could have used magic to make graves in an instant—carve them from the earth without breaking so much as a sweat. This felt better though, more natural, right. This was the way things should be.

"How is Isha?" I asked, seeing the barest bit of aura bleeding into the world around me as Jina approached.

"She would be better if you spent some time with her, but I understand," she answered, voice calm.

"I need to do this. We'll rest here tonight, and in the morning we can head to the cave. That's what you're after, isn't it?" I tried, but failed, to keep the barest hint of anger from my voice. She wasn't like Chien, who was here to help. She had her own reasons for joining us.

"Justin, you may think me cold, and perhaps I am, but I've seen this so many times. After seeing everything, it gets harder and harder to feel things the same way. It . . . builds up, only gushing out at times. You're burying those you care for? I've done that a thousand times. Losing friends? I've had hundreds I've put in the ground. When you've seen everything, it is hard to feel it again, but I am trying."

I turned to her and walked forward, sweat and soil coating me head to toe.

"You have seen nothing," I informed her. "I have seen things you can't even imagine, lost more than you can comprehend, suffered in ways you have never known."

There was a spark of fear in her eyes, an understanding. She'd seen what I could do when I wanted and knew that my words were true, but there was more—kindness buried under all the time and roughness she so often displayed.

"I believe you," she said. "And yet you are still so young." She wrapped her arms around me, patting my back gently like an old friend. "Still so very young, child. I can see it in you, the lack of years. Perhaps I'm wrong. Perhaps one day you won't become like me, or like my grandfather was. Maybe that mind of yours will keep you feeling, but feeling hurts." I seared that moment into my memory, no matter how much it hurt. I needed to remember to not drift away from my emotions. If I suffered for centuries, then so be it, but I needed to feel. Feeling kept me going, kept me moving toward something. Without it, I knew that I would just stop. Stop growing.

That evening was the burial. We couldn't bury them with their favorite things, nor say too much, since it was impossible to tell who was who. No, it was rather a quiet affair. Afterward, I gathered up some flowers, and the girls set them to growing over the graves. The roots would keep them in place, giving some new life while marking the location and keeping animals away. It felt right. Graves should have flowers, in my opinion.

CHAPTER 3

LAST OF THE ENEMY

In the morning, as we crept up to the pool's cave, we found something Jina seemed to be half expecting. Near the entrance there were a few small huts and a makeshift wall of thorns and wood. It stopped us for all of about a heartbeat. While she may not be Atal, our new companion was still very old, very powerful, and one hundred percent done with these people. The wall rotted in seconds, the few soldiers who strode out to meet us dying like dogs.

Those weren't the only ones in the camp, though. Huddled in the houses, sometimes in makeshift cages or back rooms, were women and children. The women were terrified, hiding and crying as we strode in, the children cradled in their arms.

"Hey, it's okay," I said to a few girls hiding in the first house we looked inside. "We're here to help." I extended my hand.

"Please don't hurt me, please don't hurt me," one of them mumbled, a few bruises obvious on her arms and legs.

As far as I knew, few of the other victims had been found. They'd been killed or shipped back to the Wester homeland as slaves. This was, unfortunately, expected. One of the realities of war in this world. Before I could do much to reassure the terrified girl, though, a hand landed on my shoulder.

"Justin, let Jina and I talk to them. You and Chien go and make sure there aren't any other warriors around, will you?" Isha asked.

"Of course," I agreed, realizing that I was probably not the best person for the job. "If you need us, call out."

Chien and I did as she bade us, moving to the edge of the city and keeping an eye out. It wasn't needed. Either word of the battle at Atal hadn't reached these men, or perhaps they thought they needed to run for their lives. We'd caught them all early, having barely left their beds.

"They look bad," I said to my young assistant.

"I've seen worse," he said, shrugging. I raised an eyebrow at him. "I have. They'll live, or they won't, but there's not a lot you or I can do for them right now, is there? All the villages around here are wrecked, and we're not supposed to go back to the city."

"Fair point. Don't even know what they'll want. Suppose we'll have to ask and—" A pair of screaming voices interrupted me, and it took us only a second to start running in their direction.

Two women were being ripped from one of the nicer huts in the little makeshift camp and set upon by the others. Jina and Isha stood to the side, looking displeased as a mob leapt upon them, scratching, pulling, punching. They didn't have weapons, but small hands tore at the two, dragging them about by their hair or whatever limb could be reached.

"Stop!" I said as I reached them, and was promptly ignored. "Jina," I insisted, turning to the woman, "stop them."

"They deserve what they're getting," she said coldly.

"You need to stop this. Even your grandfather would've given them a chance to make their case. You're staying, we're not. The precedent you set here and now won't go away."

She frowned at me, but she stepped forward. "Cease," she commanded, and I felt the wave of power she put forward with it. "Bring them forward."

There was muttering and angry noises, but the former captives seemed to decide that they didn't want to fight Jina. A few moments later, the pair were brought forward, kneeling, missing clumps of hair and covered in small wounds.

"You can't be thinking of letting them live!" one of the women hissed. "She killed my brother when he refused their poison!" She pointed at one of the pair.

"We have one accusation," Jina said, almost formally. "What others?"

Every one of the former captives had something to say, some of them quite a lot. The two they'd gone after were Fala and Ura, and each had a list of crimes a mile long. Both had been "preferred" by the men who'd been holding them here, and rather than being mistreated like the others, instead they helped the soldiers—helped kill some of those who had disobeyed and held down several of the girls while the soldiers did what soldiers were known to do, a betrayal few of these women were going to forgive.

"Do you have anything to say? Anything which might excuse your actions?" Jina asked, having slipped into the role of judge. Neither had spoken, nor had they been permitted to speak as the others made their cases.

Fala looked up at her. "You know what they'd have done if we hadn't," she said.

"Yes, but you would have lived. Instead you chose to harm others for comfort." Jina had not an ounce of mercy in her voice.

"Please," Ura begged. "I-I am with child."

There was a long pause, silence taking the small section of forest for ponderous moments. Of all the things that she could have said, that might have been the only one that would spare her life. Our society loved children too much. Even the child of a traitor would often be spared. A baby? No, harming such would be unthinkable.

"If you are lying, you will suffer," Jina warned her.

"I'm not," she said with a quivering voice.

The elder extended her hand, and there was a soft glow between it and Ura's body, after which she sighed.

"Truth, and it survived the beating she received." She looked to Fala. "Strangle that one. The other will live until her child is born. Then she shall share the same fate." Jina produced a vine for them with a wave of her hand and left them to it.

"Watch," the one who took up the cord told Ura, who was still being held.

They killed Fala slowly, holding her so she couldn't move as the vine was wrapped around her neck just tight enough so that she couldn't breathe. Several of the mob shot malicious looks at Ura, who was being forced to observe. When it was finally over, the woman who'd done the strangling came close.

"For when your turn comes," she hissed as she tied the vine around Ura's throat. The prisoner being able to do little more than whimper in fear.

As they dispersed, Chien leaned in and whispered, "Women are fucking scary sometimes."

"They can be very unforgiving," I said, "and quite vindictive too sometimes. Don't forget that. Can you really blame them, though?"

"Fair point."

The girls were still giving the two of us a rather wide berth. They might understand that we weren't there to hurt them, but pain took time to heal, and some of it would never go away completely.

Jina came to us after dealing with the prisoner and the corpse. "Good call," she said.

"Have the sky and ground switched places?" Chien asked in mock confusion, this world not yet having adages about pigs flying or hell freezing over. For his effort, he received an unamused look through half-lidded eyes.

"We have other things to do though," she said, pointing toward the cave.

"That we do."

CHAPTER 4

UNDERGROUND ONCE MORE

Jina walked next to me as we descended, slowly, carefully, into a place I never wanted to be again. Every step made me hurt, made my heart ache, an ache for the destruction this place had caused. Jina was silent, as if it made her too contemplative, at least until the first of the bubbles drifted forward.

"What is that?" she asked, almost panicked as she brought her hands up before her.

"Nothing to worry about," I said, pulled from my thoughts. "They've always been here—some kind of weird aura or something."

"An aura? Like the light that surrounds us?"

"Yes."

"It looks . . . almost like yours," she said accusingly.

"Yes, it does."

I kept moving forward, letting the light from mosses and mushrooms guide my way. Now was not the time to pester me. Jina, however, kept shooting me looks I could see and feel.

There'd once been a massive underground sea, but it was gone now. Either through magic or pure manpower it had been filled, the beasts lairing within it presumably killed. However, many blockages had been placed in the way. Nothing that could stop us, but enough to slow us down.

It seemed like such a long way. Without magic to power our steps or push us forward, it took so much time to make it. Our steps echoed against the walls, while the pale glowing patches and bubbles guiding us seemed to invite, or rather call us downward.

Eventually we came to the final chamber. I doubted I would ever get over the scope of it—the massive underground crater, the powerful magic in the air, the vines that so reminded me of that day I'd died. In the back of my mind, I could remember it like it was moments ago—the pain as my flesh was burned away.

Jina moved forward, stepping among the vines. She carefully reached down, and though I couldn't tell what she was doing, there was certainly some magic there.

"I cannot affect them," she declared after a few moments, then tried ripping a leaf between her fingers.

The vine did not respond—it didn't rip, didn't break, didn't seem to care about what she did. She put in more and more effort, but nothing came of it.

"Odder and odder," I said.

"Tell me, and the truth, are you of this place?" she said, moving over to one of the skeletons and moving the vines aside so she could see the skeleton.

"Could you clarify?" I asked.

"Your power is similar, your behavior odd as well. Are you the guardian or child of these plants? Are you something else?"

"I am an elf," I responded. "I was born in the village we passed through to parents who dwelt there, not in this place, not of these vines. Perhaps I'm odd, perhaps this place affected me, but if so, I don't know how, nor why."

If I outright lied, she might have some way of knowing, some spell that told her about my body's reaction. So I didn't. I didn't understand it, I didn't know why, or even what these were, nor where they'd come from. So many questions.

She looked at the pool, at the eggs from which this power flowed.

"Stranger, eggs for sure, but to what? These creatures?" she pointed at the skeleton. "Or whatever killed them?"

"I'm more concerned about what will happen with them," I told her.

"I will seal this place for now, as best I can. Then I will build a home above it and keep any away who dare trespass."

"You won't try to destroy it?" I asked.

"No. Something in my gut tells me that doing so would bring danger."

I hadn't felt that, but then again I'd never tried to destroy it. Perhaps it was like the trap I'd been stuck in. Perhaps there were other defenses, deep down in it. I didn't know, and for now I didn't need to. Perhaps one day I would return to work out the mysteries if I could, perhaps not, but for now her suggestion would do. I did have one question, though.

"What do you think will happen when the eggs hatch?" I asked.

"Nothing good."

Neither of us wanted to get too close to the water, so after she was satisfied at what she'd found we slowly made our way back to the surface. On the way, the barriers were rebuilt and fortified. Jina could make roots as strong as steel and as thick as my thigh in a hurry, and I made walls that were actually walls by manipulating the stone into place, sealed tightly so that nothing could get through. At each of the places where the tunnel got thinner, a new barrier was formed, a new stopping point for anything trying to get down here.

As we returned and saw the women, along with Isha and Chien, I looked to Jina. "Hey, so about them."

"I'll do what I can for them. I imagine some will want to go home, but some might stay here, or nearby for now. Do you care if they resettle the old village?"

"No, so long as the graves aren't disturbed," I told her.

"Things will be done with respect," she assured me.

"Um, excuse me," said a high voice, the child it belonged to approaching us.

"Yes?" I asked, since she was clearly looking at me.

"Is-is it true that you killed Cino?" she said, asking about the leader of the army who'd done all this.

"Yes," I said solemnly.

"Thank you."

"You're welcome."

"I'm Era," she told me. "If one day I can help you, let me know."

I didn't know how to respond to that. An offer of aid from one so small. I doubted I'd ever call that favor in, but being disrespectful wouldn't help.

"Very well, Era. Thank you."

With a small bow she left us, turning and running back to the women.

CHAPTER 5

THE GREAT FOREST

It had been days since we left the old village, and still we were finding destruction. Places that had clearly been abandoned in haste or destroyed. There were few bodies, those having been reclaimed by the forest in most places. Paths were also overgrown, lost amidst the war.

Our directions were . . . vague at best, the general area we needed to travel toward. Normally we'd have sought information from the villages as we passed, but without their knowledge, we only had a rough reckoning, and that was limited.

"What's that?" Chien asked.

"An iron needle that I've changed a bit," I said. "It'll help us when we can't see as well." There were clouds forming above us, so now was a pretty good time for it.

"What's it do?" he inquired, leaning close.

"If allowed to move freely, it will point north."

"Huh, that's neat."

He'd seen me use magnetism before, and the items themselves weren't unknown in this world. Naturally occurring magnets, or those made by magical creatures, existed and were rare, perhaps, but not novel. There might even have been some people who understood enough to make basic compasses. Chien might also be numb to the fact that I came up with new things all the time, but not everyone was.

"An iron needle?" said Isha as she drew in. "Like for sewing?"

"You could use it for that . . ." I said, looking at it. There was no hole for thread, but otherwise it would work.

She picked it up and looked at it for a moment.

"Too small," she finally declared. "Far too small, and no way to put on sinew or cord. Even the stuff Ida was making wouldn't work, even if there was a hole. Maybe for something else, but not for sewing."

"Guess I'll just have to keep using it to find north then," I said, pleased that she wouldn't be asking me for a bunch of them right now. I could've made them, but this wasn't the best place for experimenting, or working iron.

Our journey continued, and it was oddly peaceful. The sleeping arrangements weren't much to my liking, with Chien staying with me and Isha, preventing anything from happening at night, but he was a wise enough young man to give us some time alone every now and then. With only the three of us, we could move fast, taking game or the like as we wanted, or just asking Isha to make us some food periodically.

My significant other soon began to resent our requests for sustenance, and the fact that she couldn't make many different dishes also grated on all of us. It was another incentive to move quickly and find what we could; but, as weeks passed, some of our favorite plants became a little less common.

Oddly, it didn't get colder. I'd always associated the north with being cold. Years and years I'd spent as a resident of the deep south, watching the weather and declaring that it sucked to live in the northern section of the country. Here, however, it remained mostly the same. Sure, if we got really close to one of the mountains nearby, there was a noticeable drop in temperature, but as long as we stuck to the forests, it was pretty much always the same.

The fauna, however, did change drastically. It seemed that mile by mile the trees and plants grew. It was subtle enough to miss at first, but when every tree began looking like it was centuries older than what you were used to, you began to take heed. As we took to rest by a small creek it struck me that some of these trees would give the redwoods of earth a run for their money.

That night we found shelter in a fallen and hollow mammoth of wood. It was dry, clean, and the bugs weren't any worse than they were elsewhere. Overall, the location was pretty nice compared to some of the places we'd rested. The worst was when it rained, leaving us with little shelter. Soon the rainy season would be upon us, and I'd rather be up into the mountains when that arrived, easier to avoid any flooding.

"Justin!" called Chien around midnight. "Need you here." I quickly made my way to the spot he was using to keep watch and noticed that he wasn't alone. There were around a dozen elves with spears, shields of bark and vine, and unhappy looks upon their faces. They weren't in an aggressive stance just yet, but it was clear they didn't want to be here. Rather than the leathers we favored, they were dressed in clothes sewn together from some kind of leaves.

"You are trespassing," their leader declared, stepping forward. "As we told the others, you cannot seek shelter here." It was clear from the small shock of white hair on his head that he was the elder of this group.

"We have spoken to no others," I began, before a raised hand cut me off.

"Perhaps it is so, and I am not without mercy, but you cannot stay. We will not get involved in the fighting between the men of Atal and the men of Cino." At that I bristled, but I understood his reasons. They didn't want war.

"That is not our purpose, nor to stay. The fighting is over. We're here to report the results to your ancient."

There was a look of understanding in his eyes and deep sadness. This man, at least, had seen enough to know that I was here to report a death, not a positive thing for our species in general. "Oh, I see. Come, we will go to the village."

"Old One? I thought we must turn them away?" one of the younger elves said, piping in.

"He is a messenger," the elder said. "He may pass." He then looked at me. "Since you appear to be a man of Atal, should I assume that he won?"

"Both fell," I reported, and there were stunned looks on more than one face in the greeting party.

That wasn't a secret, and it was my job to spread the news. There was a possibility that the news would beat me to one or more of the ancients, but that didn't matter. What mattered was the ceremony. Word of their deaths was to be spread, with a designated person to tell the ancients of the loss of one of theirs.

"That . . . We will speed you along then, this news must be spread," their elder said after a full ten seconds of staring at me. "Come, there is no time to waste."

CHAPTER 6

THE PEOPLE OF THE FOREST

The local elder, called Old One by the locals, quickly escorted us to his home, and what a home it was.

The people of this forest had taken some parts of the culture I was used to, like the living trees and vines in our homes, and amped them up to eleven. Rather than simply having them as support structures, they lived in the trees themselves, houses grown from the plants around them. Bridges of vine connected platforms of living wood between the giants they were suspended in.

While I liked my home, this place much more resembled the ideas that most people of earth would have associated with my kind. It was clear that there was some sort of connection here, something more at play, but I didn't yet know what.

The village was obvious once we grew near, and I was sure that from the air it would be even more so. Each of the trees here was far larger than the surrounding ones, with the centerpiece being more akin to a miniature skyscraper than something formed from normal wood.

"That's some kind of tree," Chien commented.

"I planted it when I first became a man, as is our tradition. The others of the village were the same, but not mine; rather my kin's," the old elf informed us.

"Interesting tradition," I said. "Is that why all the trees here are so large?"

"In part. When we are able we have those whose power blooms within them strengthen the trees or shape them, growing them larger and larger as we age. Similarly, when we die, the trees are no longer strengthened and will instead eventually join us in death," he explained as we made our way to a ladder.

The elder went up first, along with his people, followed by Chien. I briefly looked at Isha and gave a mischievous smile, only for her to point me to the ladder with an amused expression. We both knew the views we would have on the way up, as brief skin clothing sort of beat that into your system.

When she finally made it to the top Isha asked the elder, "So the others are from your family?"

"Yes, and that was my sister's tree," he said indicating one close to the large central behemoth. "My cousin, my grand-niece." He pointed out others as we moved about. "Most are gone now, but are honored by those who've taken up residence in their trees."

When we reached his home it was fairly nice by all metrics. With the height, there was little dirt inside, and of course the floors and walls were shaped magically, so they formed more organic-looking openings. There were even some fungi that let off a soft light, glowing on what were clearly brought-in logs, rather than the tree itself.

"So, what happened to the ancients?" one of the others asked as we came in, as a few of the locals brought food for us.

"There was a great battle at the city. They fought, and others fought as well. When it was all over, Cino killed Atal, only to be felled by one of our leader's comrades," I said. It was the truth, even if I wasn't taking credit, though nonspecific enough that I didn't anticipate any issues.

"Is the one who put down Cino taking over as the new leader?" the same man asked in response.

"No, we are now without an ancient. Do you think it likely any of your people will . . ." I didn't even finish before he began shaking his head.

"We prefer to stay in our forest, and I doubt any of the oldest will change what they want."

I shrugged. Perhaps some of the others wanted an ancient around, but I didn't much care for them. If there were things we needed them for, it might be better to just improve tactics and weapons. My opinion was that they would be better in the long run than with one potent leader who could otherwise do whatever they wanted.

"We understand," I said. "If it is not too much to ask, could you point us in the direction of the fastest way to the ancient?" I asked.

"I will provide you with a guide and some food for part of the way, since clearly you're unused to this place," he said with a laugh. Fair enough. We really didn't know our way around. "And also some advice—travel in the afternoon and seek shelter high. There are few beasts in the forest, but those that are here are difficult to battle. Between that and the rains, you do not want to be on the ground at night."

His piece spoken, he invited us to eat, and we got to try the local foods. They were wildly different than what I was used to—hardly any roots or berries and few meats. Much of what was brought looked something like a breadfruit, large and round, seared on the outside. With it came a number of other more familiar fruits, and a lot of salad. If they didn't go to the ground much, that made sense. Gathering leaves was easier than digging in the dirt, and perhaps the foliage was even grown up here. We were also given a number of eggs cooked in the shell—a good substitute for the otherwise missing protein.

Overall, the elder here was quite pleasant. It seemed he understood our mission and approved of it. I didn't even need to question why that was, since I was basically telling him that his border, something which for the last year or so would have been a major thorn in his side, was now as secure as it could be.

The other villagers were much more standoffish. They didn't take any action against us, but it was clear that they really wanted nothing to do with our group. I wondered why that was, but it seemed impolitic to ask, so I let it go. At any rate, we'd be out of their hair soon enough, so there was no need to stress about it.

About noon, small sacks of tough, sewn-together leaves were delivered, and we met our guide. He was shorter than me, with brown hair and sharp eyes.

"I am Rolan, son of Rylan, and Old One has asked that I guide you part of the way to the Great Tree," he announced.

"Nice to meet you. I am Justin, and this is Isha and Chien," I said, as our spokesman.

"It is considered polite to name your fathers as well," he informed us.

With a nod, Isha and I did just that, but our third member ran into a snag.

"Never met him," Chien said with a shrug.

"But certainly you know his name?" Rolan asked.

"Nope," he answered with a smile.

The guide seemed taken aback by that, almost unsure of what to say. "Then . . . did another man of your family raise you? That would be the next best answer."

"No."

It was clear that we'd thrown Rolan for a loop, and with how serious he seemed to be with his introduction, I was sure that Chien was having a blast with it.

"Then another? Certainly there has been someone."

"Closest is Justin. He started teaching me when I was still this high," Chien said, making a hand motion of about how tall he was when we first met. It was strangely accurate too.

"Then you are Chien, of the tree of Justin," Rolan said before approaching me and clapping a hand on my shoulder. "To take in a child that is of no relation to you is a noble thing."

"I don't think I deserve any merit in that," I replied, having been mostly taking in the kid for my own reasons.

"Humility too. I think I will like traveling with you, Justin."

I, on the other hand, thought it might be a chore, something the snickering behind me almost certainly confirmed.

CHAPTER 7

PATHS THROUGH THE TREES

Rolan was by no means the worst traveling companion I'd ever had, but he was certainly the most serious. He was perhaps a bit formal. Everything had to be exactly the right way all the time. Knowledgeable too, being able to show us to paths we'd never have found on our own, which arced through the trees rather than the ground. If he could just relax, we'd all have gotten along a lot better though.

"It sure seems like a lot of effort to build and maintain all these," I said as we crossed another bridge between two giants.

"Less than you'd think. The paths are alive, so just a bit of work here and there keeps them as they should be. If they were dead wood and fiber like your people use, it would be, but we prefer it this way." He made a good point. The bridges were fairly nice too, and while I didn't really love that they were something I couldn't work with, I was sure Mother and those like her would probably have appreciated it. The vines stretched between trees with an almost wicker weave for a floor. I wondered just how far this could be taken, though I also felt I was likely to find out.

"So, you just grow them? Is it really that easy?" Isha asked, and since she could work magic that I couldn't, she might well know better than I.

"Easy? No, but worth the time," Rolan answered. "Do you mind if I ask a question in return?"

"Go ahead," I offered.

"I'd like to hear about the battle, about the glorious war between the two ancients. I've never truly seen an ancient fight. It must have been amazing."

For a few moments, the crickets were the only things we could hear. Nobody spoke, but Isha and Chien looked at me, watching, waiting to see what I would say. That was good, for I truly did have my own opinions on the matter, and neither of my companions had been present for the deaths of the ancients.

"It was not glorious; it was not wonderful. Perhaps there are battles like that, battles where someone is right and they do well and there is honor, but there was none in that fight. Cino killed Atal with his magic and died shortly thereafter. In the end, there was poison on the ground, smoke in the air, and more dead younglings than I cared to ever see again," I told him.

"I . . . youths?" He seemed confused.

"Yes, our enemy used them as soldiers, poisoning them and sending them to die. By the end of it, far too many lay dead."

That made him be quiet for a time. Rolan didn't seem the worst sort, and probably held to most of the same kinds of traditions we did, but there was much he didn't know. So we passed much of that day in silence, trudging along the roads grown into the sky.

Night came eventually, and in one of the trees there was a sizable hollow. It looked like something from an old nature film, like the inside of a giant bird's nest, sans most of the nesting materials. The entrance was small and covered by a wicker door, presumably to keep wildlife out, but soon enough we'd settled inside and set up our watch.

The sun set slowly, sinking unseen until the forest was deep in darkness, and then a new life began to awaken among the underbrush. There were fireflies here and there, pulsing like a wave near the forest floor, signaling to one another. Among them, in the excess light they gave off and within the slivers of moonlight that slipped through the branches, roamed animals, mostly small critters looking for food. Even birds sang at night here, something that didn't happen much where I came from, species in this area telling others of their kind about their territory.

"It is beautiful, isn't it?" Rolan asked as he settled near me.

"Yes, almost peaceful," I agreed.

"Anything but," he chuckled. "I used to think it was peaceful, but down there they war. Each of those creatures seeks mates, or food, or to fight others of their own kind, or of different kinds. It is beautiful, but only because we watch it from so far away."

"An interesting take," I said thoughtfully.

"I offended you earlier. I apologize. Watching from afar, I thought the war you were in must have been glorious, but much like this," he said, pointing below, "it would have been much different from your perspective."

"I made weapons," I told him.

"Oh? And I took you for a soldier."

"Not normal weapons. Special ones, just for that war. I made weapons so horrid that when it was over, they asked me to take on the task of making more weapons. The people of the city fear me, I think, fear me for what I did."

"Ah, that . . . makes sense. New things can be fearful indeed, but do you regret it? Would you have held those back had you known what would happen?" he asked.

"No. I have regrets, failures of my own, but knowing what I knew then, and what I know now, I do not regret my actions."

I saw Rolan smile at me from across the little opening we sat beside. "Then put it from your mind, for we must all do things we hate. It's sometimes better than doing nothing at all, though, and knowing which is which is the most important."

"Atal was . . . Well, I won't say I trusted him, or thought him a particularly kind person, but he did some good, didn't he? His rule was at least peaceful and fair to an extent. I wonder how the city will fare without him," I mused.

"Did you know him?" Rolan asked.

"Hmm? Oh, a bit. Like I said, I made weapons, and I made some for him." I laughed. "It was almost funny. He was so excited when I got him the first prototypes and they functioned for him. I get the feeling he missed the way a spear felt in his hand, or a club. It was the most emotion I ever saw from him, if I'm to tell you the truth."

Rolan lay back. "Yes, it seems that the older one of us gets, the more we become bored by things. Elders get it bad sometimes, where they become almost like trees, hardly moving unless they must, hardly reacting. I hope I never become like that."

"Nor I, but you know, there seems to be so much in the world we don't know that I doubt I'll ever run out of topics to look into." I looked up. "Who knows, maybe one day we'll walk among the stars, having learned more secrets than we could have ever imagined."

"That, my friend, is a dream, one you should pursue. If you aim so high, I'm sure that you'll find great and wonderful things. Take care, though. Sometimes we end up doing more damage than we could imagine if we fall."

CHAPTER 8

TALKS WITH ROLAN

I thought it impossible that the flora would get bigger than it already was in those first days that Rolan traveled with us, and I was proven wrong. The trees didn't seem to get much taller, but they got thicker and wider, with branches that I could have walked down. They weren't quite the size of a city block yet, but they were easily their own small ecosystems. There were things living in them, in the little pools that gathered in the hollows, in the bark, and along their length and breadth. Most of the animals we saw up there with us were small, but they weren't the only creatures roaming about.

"I don't want to fight that," Chien said, looking where we all were.

"Agreed," I said.

"It's not a predator, so even if it sees us, it's likely to leave us be. Well, so long as we don't threaten it," Rolan pointed out, and I could see what he was talking about.

The creature in question looked almost like an elephant, though there were no tusks, and it had a thick, shaggy coat. It was also easily thrice the size of the largest elephant I'd ever seen. This creature could dwarf one. It trudged along, reaching out now and then to rip up a low-lying piece of vegetation and eat it, munching on ferns and vines that were easily as large as I was.

"Even those that eat plants can be pretty nasty if you anger them," I pointed out, remembering the stories of moose from Earth.

"True, but we're not planning on fighting it, are we?" Isha asked.

"If you do, I'm not helping," Chien said with a shake of his head.

At any rate, the creature was a couple hundred feet below us. I certainly wasn't going to go and irritate it, and none of our companions seemed keen to either. Of course, I did have some questions.

"No, we'll leave it be. Though, Rolan, do your people ever hunt them? I imagine that one would provide quite the amount of food."

"Sometimes," he answered. "Though generally only at the end of the mating season. The males that lose fights over females will be injured and can be taken down without too much trouble, assuming enough powerful individuals come together. Sadly while there's a good bit of meat on them, it is rather tough, not something I'd recommend."

As days passed, we skirted the territories of some of the other villages. The center of the forest was still some ways away, and we didn't want trouble with any others. Night after night darkness came, washing over the world, and each night I found myself in deep conversation with Rolan.

"You wish to see a world where there is plenty?" he asked.

"Yes, though more than that, a world where our people are safe," I replied.

"Our?"

"Yes, our, all of us. Not just those who live in the coastal forest, or the great northern one. Even Cino's people who live upon the plains. A better world for each and every one of us, where children can be safe and monsters do not hunt our kind."

He chuckled. "That is a pleasant dream, but I doubt it will ever come to be."

"It may not," I agreed. Certainly Earth had its fair share of problems. "But even if things are better than they are now, that is something. Even if the goal we seek is unreachable, I still think the seeking is worth something, is it not?"

"I suppose, and even my people have worked toward that. Progress is slow, but I've been told that before our ancient took power the forest was a much darker, dangerous place, with fearsome beasts that no longer roam here. Nowadays, there are far fewer monsters to hunt us, and we live in relative peace. The fruits also grow bigger, though nobody is sure why."

"Hm? Oh, that's likely because people protect and plant more seeds from the best tasting ones," I said, stretching.

"How should that matter?" he asked. "Do you think the new ones remember the old?"

"No, nothing like that. It's just that if a vine produces tasty fruit, then it will be propagated. Most or all of its descendants will be similar, but then if another one tastes just a bit better, then that will become the vine people want to grow. Continue this for many generations and they'll improve."

I didn't bother going into the deeper parts of evolution with him, but that basic concept was simple enough for anyone to understand.

"But how does it know what to make?" he asked.

"It doesn't need to. Look, children look like their parents right?" I asked.

"Sure."

"It's like that, but with fruit, or leaves, and over many, many generations. Small changes heaped one on top of another that lead to slightly larger changes."

There was a look in Rolan's eyes. Something odd. He looked as if he understood, but he wanted more, more understanding, to know why I thought this way.

"What makes you think this is so?" he finally asked.

"Experience," I answered.

"Odd," he said. "You're an odd one, Justin, a very odd one. You're young. I can tell that by how you move, but you also feel . . . old, older than you should be."

"Atal thought much the same," I admitted.

"I imagine he did. I'm sure our ancient will want to talk to you at length, and don't think that he'll let you get away without telling him exactly how Atal came to perish either. My understanding is that the two were, if not friends, at least well known to one another."

"Yeah, one of Atal's people said they got along well. His granddaughter, Jina. I rather like her, even if she's rough around the edges sometimes," I said, leaning back.

"Is she the one taking over for Atal?" he asked. "I was of the understanding that nobody had."

"No, she's . . . doing other things, things she feels she must. Personally, I think if she tried, most people would accept it, but she doesn't seem to want to. I get that too. Leading is probably no fun at all."

That set him to laughing. "No Justin, leading is seldom enjoyable."

While I was supposed to be up and watching, I found myself strangely tired. Rolan gave me a motion that I could rest, and within moments my eyes shut, letting me drift off to sleep.

CHAPTER 9

THE GREAT TREE

Though our journey wasn't that long, I liked to think Rolan and I became friends. That was something I'd had few of in either life, but he was inquisitive, decent, and generally interested in what others thought, and that went a long way with me. I answered his questions where I could, but there were some things I still wasn't willing to share with anyone.

"Tomorrow we'll be in sight of the Great Tree," he informed us as we ate dinner, a mixture of food Isha had summoned and some greens Rolan had shown us.

"Glad to hear it," Chien said through a mouthful of food. "I'm looking forward to seeing what you guys have for a city, and spending tomorrow night there will be something to look forward to."

"Agreed, and we're almost out of supplies," Isha pointed out. She'd taken to managing that aspect of our journey, similar to how she'd helped with running my home back before we'd left Atal.

"Um, no," Rolan said with a shake of his head.

"No?" I asked.

"No, we'll not be resting in the settlement tomorrow. I'd explain, but it'll be easier to just show you in the morning."

The rest of us just shrugged. He'd been an excellent guide through the forest so far, and we had no reason to worry about waiting until dawn to see. Perhaps the settlement was visible from far off, the center standing out from the surroundings, or maybe we'd be on a hill or something. I really didn't know what the underlying ground was doing, having spent so long in the treetops. We rose well before dawn, Rolan thinking we should get into position, so we walked in the cool morning darkness. I summoned a number of magical lights to guide us—simple glowing orbs—and show the way as Rolan moved us into position. Before too long we found the place and our direction changed.

As the patches of sky visible through the thick canopy began to lighten, we climbed. It was clear that we weren't the first, stairs and simple rails growing from the tree we were ascending. Step by step we reached upward, like the branches all around us, aiming for the sky. Even in the excellent shape we were all currently in, we were also quite tired by the time we made it, bursting forth from the shade of the leaves and onto a bough that grew above the surrounding limbs.

"So, what are we looking at?" Chien asked, looking around.

"The largest tree in the forest," Rolan said pointing toward what appeared to be a mountain.

"Is it on that mountain?" my young apprentice asked, making me shake my head, though even I didn't want to believe it.

"No, it is that mountain," I said, trying to fathom what I was seeing.

You'd be forgiven for missing it at first, but that particular plant was . . . impossible in size. I couldn't make out the branches, or what was on them, but the thing had to be a mile high. There were low-lying clouds around it, and it seemed to just blend in with its surroundings, like it was meant to be there. Smaller trees grew all around it, giants surely, but nothing compared to the mammoth. Heck, it wouldn't surprise me if there were a good few growing under it as well.

I'd have to check, but as Rolan had pointed out, not today. It was far, and our movement through the forest wasn't exactly fast most of the time. Trudging through bridges and over old limbs wasn't quick, and it wasn't like there was a river for boats or anything. Then again, with flora and fauna this large, I'd hate to see what kinds of monsters would live in any body of water.

"Magnificent," Isha said, earning her a small smile from Rolan.

"It is, isn't it. I never get tired of seeing it in its full glory."

"Have you been here many times?" I asked.

"Oh, a good few over my years." I'd known he was older than me, but not how much. Less than a hundred years, presumably, since he had none of the white hairs we gained at such an age.

As we got closer and closer, it was clear that the paths were more maintained, the trees more curated. That wasn't to say there were tons of people about, as it was another day and a half before we met another elf on one of the paths between the trees.

"Hail, strangers," he said as he approached, packs bulging all over his body. He was clearly a trader of some kind.

"Greetings," I said, nodding. "Hard journey?"

"Oh, no better or worse than any other, and just starting out." He began setting down his burdens and stretching, looking us over. "Please, call me Layen. So, anything in particular you're looking for?"

"We were going to wait until we got to the center . . ." Chien demurred, looking toward us.

Layen looked almost shocked, eyes going between each of us. "You're from far away. I can tell by your clothes, but surely you won't leave me without some exchange?"

Rolan coughed. "It's considered bad luck for a trader to not have some business with those he meets if he's more than a day from any settlement. Indicates that the other side doesn't trust him, or means him harm. Even an exchange of stories is enough, if you have nothing else."

"Yes, yes," the man nodded. "Even if it's not much." He gave an odd look to Rolan, but then returned his gaze to the rest of us.

"I've got a few beads I could part with if you've something to make our dinner more interesting," Isha offered.

Back in Atal beads were the medium of exchange, with rarer types and materials acting as larger denominations of the local currency. What Isha offered were some of the cheapest from the city, though—small shells similar to cowrie, and not even colorful ones. It seemed she didn't expect much from this exchange.

"Oh, those are interesting. Use them in your hair and stuff? Novel. Not sure how people will take to it, but I'm sure we can come up with something for it."

"Is wearing such things not common around here?" Almost everyone back home had some worked into their outfits somewhere, and women who were well-off flaunted their wealth with them.

"Not really, no," Layen answered.

"Then what do people decorate themselves with?" Isha asked, tilting her head. Seems she'd never really considered other options.

"Oh, feathers, bits of shell worked into clothing, if you can get it, and you can tell someone's really well-off if their clothes are grown, you know, all the leaves perfectly shaped. Takes skill to do that right, but almost nobody wastes their time."

I was finding this all very interesting. Each culture had its small differences, even if we were close enough to all speak the same language. Chien had other thoughts, though, and elbowed me before leaning in to speak close.

"Boss, should we worry about funds? I didn't bring much other than beads to trade with."

I just smiled. "No, I've got some ideas," I answered as Isha pulled a few small herbs from the man, looking rather pleased with what she'd managed to get.

CHAPTER 10

ASCENT OF THE TREE

Unlike the city of Atal, where there was a wall, here in the forest there were no such things. That didn't mean there weren't guards, though. There were, and we were certainly stopped well before we got to the shade cast by the arboreal king that dominated this region. Most of them only took a few moments to look us over and ask basic questions, though, and since we were a small group with a woman and youth in tow, it was clear we weren't here to make trouble.

Once we were under the branches themselves I couldn't stop looking. There were houses and businesses grown from the thick bark, pulled up with even more plants atop them. More than that, though, were the clouds.

"It has its own weather," I remarked, looking at the condensation hanging in the air.

"Oh yes," Rolan confirmed. "Particularly at this time, near the rainy season, this place is unbearably wet."

"Why?" asked Isha. Outside the branches there were no clouds this low.

"Water evaporates, like your hair drying," I replied, "and when it does, it goes into the air. From there it moves about into the sky to fall again as rain. However, with the leaves covering it here, it cannot escape. It acts like the roof of a hut, keeping smoke or, in this case, water in."

All of them looked at me, and I realized that once again I'd said something strange.

"I've . . . never heard it put like that," Rolan said, giving me a questioning look.

"Justin's weird," Chien answered.

"But normally right," my lover added.

"Yes, normally right," I said. For the time being, that seemed to satisfy Rolan, but I made a mental note to keep my mouth shut around him for just a bit longer.

Some of the bridges here were getting to truly impressive sizes, living vines and wood were only so strong. As we approached one, moving us to a branch with something akin to a road on it, I bent down to look, letting a few drops of the forming rain bounce off the back of my neck.

"See something, boss?" Chien asked.

"These shouldn't work," I said.

"And why not?" our guide asked, seemingly offended.

"Look at the size, Rolan. They're massive, and plants are only so strong. Is something done to strengthen them?" There had to be magic worked into them somewhere. Either a special type of plant or something else. I just couldn't work out what.

"Old One back in the village did some things to make the vines there stronger, so probably. I'm sure we could ask someone, but how did you know?"

"Rolan, I've built a lot of things. Not a lot of bridges, but a lot of things, and there's a certain point where all materials stop working. A short crossing made of plants is one thing—they can do that no problem. This one will hold at least a thousand, and four people could walk along it beside one another. That's different, and I don't think most plants could handle that; their own weight would be a problem."

"And you don't trust them?" Rolan inquired.

"Oh, I'm sure they work; I just want to know how. Would help for when I'm building things in the future."

After a few minutes I decided that it was both a question for later and one I hadn't the expertise for right now. I wasn't really a plant guy—just thought they were neat—and I'd wasted enough time on it. We also had several people stopping to look at us strangely, and we weren't really here to cause a ruckus, so it was time to keep going.

It took over an hour to reach the trunk of the central tree, and when we did I was still stunned. The size simply couldn't be overstated. It was surreal, almost like looking at something from a painting. It put to shame anything from Atal, or that I'd seen in this world so far, and gave me some hope that there were many new discoveries to be had.

A path had been grown for those going up or down, stretching and winding between the different branches and their districts, and we began to climb. Going a mile up didn't seem like too big a deal, until we realized that we weren't going straight up. To keep the incline manageable, the ramp wasn't that steep, meaning it was long, miles and miles long of circling the massive tree, seeming almost to go up by mere inches.

"Don't suppose you know a way to fly, Justin?" Chien asked, looking tired.

"I've got some ideas, but none that are immediately helpful."

"On flying?" Isha and Rolan chorused.

"None that are immediately helpful. Are you sure we have to go up all the way, Rolan?" It had been him who'd led us here, and he didn't look as bothered by the hike as the rest of us.

"The ancient resides on the highest level, not quite the very top of the tree, but close. Being high and above others indicates how close to him you are."

Looks like the idea of "having a view" was multiversal too. I couldn't really blame him, the ruler of this place could probably have things brought straight to him if he wanted, and seeing the whole forest from that height had to be beautiful.

"I'm sure we could find you a mountain or a massive tree to live in one day, Justin," Chien needled, seeing my thoughtfulness on the subject.

"Nah, never really liked being too high up. Pretty to see, but not where I'd want to live."I had to give it to the locals; even if I thought their idea of living like this was weird, they did at least put plenty of sitting areas along the path for those ascending to take breaks on. It'd be necessary for people who didn't have body-based magic or weren't able to just hurl themselves through the sky by some method or another. By the fourth hour, though, I was sorely tempted to try and figure out how to fly. If not for me, then for Isha. She looked miserable.

"Please tell me we're nearly there," she griped.

"Almost, but we might want to wait here a little longer. If you're not in a rush?" Rolan said.

"Not horribly, but why?" I returned.

"You'll see."

It was already late, and the sun beginning to set, so we took a longer break to have a little picnic. Even this high up there was plenty of room, and since these areas were specifically for rests, nobody cared. As darkness fell I began to see what Rolan meant.

Slowly, quite slowly at first, the dark places below us began to shine. In the shadows near us I saw them too—flowers and vines that emitted a pale radiance of various colors. It wasn't bright, not the strong light of a fire, but it was more than enough to see by. I'd not noticed it on the way here, the leaves shielding the glow, but now, below me the branches and homes began to stand out.

"No fires, just . . . plants?" Chien said, looking below us at the shimmering lights.

"It gets dry. Fire would be dangerous, but these," Rolan nodded.

I was glad we'd stopped like he suggested. Perhaps I wasn't much for views, but this one was certainly rather breathtaking.

CHAPTER 11

ANOTHER ANCIENT

When we finally reached the top of the tree we were greeted by a several guards. They looked us over as if waiting for what we had to say.

"I am a messenger from the lands of Atal, here to deliver news to your ancient," I declared.

After a few more moments of staring, one sighed. "Come in, please."

Even at the top of this absolute monster of a plant there was a ton of room. It was also clear that the inside was almost completely hollow. That didn't make a lot of sense with what I knew about plants, but who knew what sort of nonsense a powerful magus could come up with if they had centuries to think it over. It did make me wonder how this tree grew, though. Questions I could ask if it came up.

There were rooms, and we were shown to one, not carved or cut, but simply a part of the tree, grown fully from the wood. It even had a few places to sit, with woven branches for softer spots and a small risen table to wait at.

And wait we did. An hour passed while our group sat there, doing nothing. Perhaps the local ancient was busy, or sleeping, or just didn't want to see us. It rankled me, though, being made to wait like this.

"Mind if I go talk to the guards?" Rolan suggested. "Maybe see what's going on?"

"Go for it," I encouraged. I may not have known proper procedure, but perhaps he knew some way to speed things up.

He did, and after a few moments of whispering, which I didn't bother trying to listen in on, he shot me a smile.

"I'll be back a little later," he told me.

"Look, Rolan, be careful. I knew Atal fairly well, and he wasn't one to suffer fools. If the ancient doesn't want to deal with you, or tells you to go away, do it."

He patted my shoulder and thanked me for the advice before leaving with one of the guards. Shortly afterward, we were told that we wouldn't be seen tonight, but that we could sleep in the room we were in. That was a bit bothersome, but having a roof over my head was nice. Would have been better if they'd provided a proper area to sleep, though, or some privacy.

"Is he coming back?" Chien asked as Isha pulled in close to me and curled up.

"It's fine," she assured him. "If they wanted us hurt, they wouldn't need to wait."

That wasn't reassuring, but what did help was our guide returning in the middle of the night. I'd just woken up to relieve Chien of the guard rotation, something we were maintaining regardless, and he quietly strode in, a smile on his face and a small basket of fruit under one arm.

"Everything well?" I quietly inquired.

"No problems. Just needed to explain some things; we even got some snacks." He passed me a piece of fruit, a small almost citrus-like thing.

"Thanks, it's been good traveling with you." The snack was sour, quite so, but I didn't mind.

"You too, Justin."

"After we deliver the message, well, we're off to the west. Going to try and go around Cino's lands and get to the plateaus up there. From my understanding, that's the next ancient."

"I've heard of her," Rolan said. "She's . . . Well, she probably won't hurt you without cause, but those folks are supposed to be pretty rough."

"Want to come? If you don't have anything else going on, we'd love to have you."

He chuckled. "I appreciate the offer, but sadly I can't run off to circle the world with you."

"Well enough, though, I think you'd have enjoyed it. If you change your mind."

"I'll let you know."

From there, we did our normal nightly ritual lightly chatting until it was his turn for watch. It was nice, and even if our journey together was coming to an end, it wasn't like there was no chance of us meeting again. We lived long, long lives, and so friendships could come and go. It wasn't even like there was a rush.

The next morning a guard came to get us. She seemed pleasant, if formal, and didn't seem bothered that we weren't really in the best of conditions. It would've been nice if we'd been given something more than the fruit from the night before for breakfast, but I didn't anticipate that the ancient was pleased to hear his friend was dead, assuming word had made it before we did.

We went back outside, circling the tree a couple more times before finally coming to another little entry. The interior was decorated with glowing plants, vines, and fruit trees, all melded into the wood of the Great Tree. In the center was, of course, a throne. It seemed ancients liked thrones, and it fit them, almost king-like in their ways, rulers of our kind. I wondered briefly if criminals were brought here like they were before Atal. The throne was empty, its owner missing. There were guards, servants, and aides, but the ruler himself was gone, missing. I looked around, but they all just stood there, waiting, watching.

"What's going on?" Chien whispered.

By way of answering, Rolan stepped forward, one hand coming up to run through his hair. As he did so, it changed, the color fading, stripping away. I couldn't take my eyes off of it, watching his locks change to pure white as he turned, taking his seat.

"My apologies for the deception," the ancient said, smiling slightly. "You see, I needed to get home anyway, and learning what I could on the way seemed entertaining. Now, let us talk about what happened in Atal, and who exactly killed whom, and how."

CHAPTER 12

A BRIEF GOODBYE

Rolan, whom I'd traveled halfway across these lands with, smiled at me from atop his wooden throne. He seemed at peace, satisfied with how things were going, and was waiting for me to respond.

"So, is your name actually Rolan? Or was that a farce?" I asked lightly.

I heard the gritting of teeth from some of those here with us, but the ancient just laughed, throwing his head back.

"See, that's what I like about you," said the ancient. "You're . . . different. Too few would dare to make a joke like that, even my own people, even the ones I like. It is Rolan, by the way, but few use it."

The guards who'd visibly tensed loosened, though a few still glared at me. It was something to disrespect him here and now, even a little. This was his place, his home, his palace, and I had no doubts that if he wanted to, he could kill me with little effort.

"Well . . . I suppose that I've done my duty and delivered my message then. Though you said you wanted clarification?"

"Yes, who killed Atal, truly?"

"Cino," I said. "He managed to get Atal stuck in the air, and that was it," I answered easily, it was the truth.

"Believable. I've never seen an ancient fall that way, but others have. I'm sad to hear it, but what is done is done. The real question, though, is who killed Cino?" He stared at me, eyes boring into mine.

"I did, with a one-use weapon."

"What kind?"

"Made of magical crystals, not exactly something one finds sitting around."

His eyes went wide and he leaned back. "That's certainly effective, well, depending on the type of crystal . . ."

"He deserved it after the number of children he killed. Mind if I ask a question, though?" I didn't want him thinking too hard on where I'd gotten such a weapon, or if I could make one again. While I didn't think he'd meant me any ill will, it was still best to avoid that question.

"Go ahead."

"Why were you at the edge of your territory? It doesn't seem like a coincidence."

Rolan laughed. "Oh yes, I was hearing of the increasing issues at the border. While I didn't want to, I did need to consider that I'd have to act. If Cino won, or if he turned his eyes toward our lands next, my presence there would have been necessary."

I sighed. "We really could have used the aid."

"It was not my place to interfere in the doings of Atal's lands. There are few of us, and even though I liked him, that might have ended up with us in conflict. We avoid conflict most of the time; that is how we make it to our ages." Rolan seemed almost saddened by that, but I got the feeling it was the truth.

Atal didn't, as far as I knew, ask for any help. Perhaps if he had, Rolan would have sent some form of aid, but that would have displayed weakness, a weakness that would have invited other challengers that he surely didn't want. It also would have put Rolan at risk for a fight that didn't benefit his people at all. Surely neither of them wanted the trouble, and so they kept separate about it.

"Now I have a question," Rolan said. "Why did you despise Cino so much?"

"He used horrid tactics, destroyed all that stood before him, and on a personal note, destroyed my village. I had many reasons to oppose him."

"But why did you?" he asked once more.

I took some time to think on that. I'd hated him, but for so many reasons. Sure, Atal had come to me for aid against him, but I wanted it to. Was it for the children? Perhaps if he'd just killed a bunch of kids, I'd have fled. Was it that pool? While I certainly didn't want people messing with it, I would wager there was only so much they could do.

"He killed my family," I finally answered, the pain in my heart knowing that I would never see my parents or childhood friends again.

Rolan leaned back once more, tapping the arms of his throne. "Yes, that is a good reason to oppose someone."

He looked back at my companions, addressing Isha first. "Though we've interacted little, thank you for joining these two."

"Justin needs someone to look after him, else he'll do stupid things like not eat," she replied with a smile.

"You too, Chien," Rolan said. "You've much growing to do, but I think this journey will help."

"Of course it will. Boss knows his stuff. Nice tree, by the way," he joked.

"Thank you. I planted it when I was young, and I must say, it has grown better than I could have ever hoped. An old friend and family member of sorts." He seemed to find the comment at least somewhat amusing.

The old elf turned back to me, still smiling. "I enjoyed our time traveling, and while I'll still have to deny joining you for the rest of your journey, I'll extend this invitation. When you are finished, you are welcome to return here. I'm sure that I can find a place for you."

"Thank you," I said. "I'll keep it in mind." I doubted I'd ever really want to join this nation, but it was clear that he meant it.

"In the meantime, I'll have my people prepare you some supplies to ease your trip."

With that, we were released. Perhaps he wanted more, perhaps he didn't care. After all, I was sure that he'd seen more than I could imagine. I got the feeling that while he liked me, our grouped ranked far lower on his priorities now that he knew there was no direct threat and that Cino hadn't been killed by someone aiming for him too. Then again, what did I know of the priorities of a millennia–old king? Not much other than that he seemed a bit more relaxed and less bored than the last one I'd met.

We were shown back to the guest room, now deprived of our formerly missing party member. In the time we'd been gone, a feast had been arranged with plenty of fruits and vegetables, and even a good bit of meat. All of us dug in, particularly on the meat, since we'd been horribly lacking in the protein department for the last few days.

CHAPTER 13

LIFT

The morning after our meeting with Ancient Rolan we were brought two packs and a selection of supplies. Here came our first surprise, for among the gear brought to us were several garments that looked almost like large coats, sewn from the hides of long-haired animals. There were also blankets of a similar make.

"Those are going to be heavy," griped Chien.

"If Rolan sent these to us, he must think we'll need them," I said.

"He probably knows something about where we're going," agreed Isha. "They are going to be heavy, though, and the packs as well.

The packs she indicated were large blankets sewn from some similar material, though without hair, clearly meant to be folded up into sacks. They weren't loaded yet, and we'd been brought a selection of dried foods and some basic tools, things that might help us. Overall, there was too much for us to carry everything, but some of it at least would be easy to bring.

After thinking for a while, I turned to one of the attendants and said,

"Excuse me, would it be possible to get some wood? Straight pieces about this long? Also a bit of twine?" I indicated a few lengths with my hands, and she nodded. After all, I'd not asked for anything complex.

Over the next hour I built frames, getting some small strips of materials to make into belts and straps. Basic sacks were easy to make, but proper framed backpacks, even improvised ones, would be a lot better for us to take a larger amount of supplies. This was something I'd not bothered with before, but with the extra size and clothing, simpler bags wouldn't do, and I had a feeling that if we left those coats behind, we'd sorely regret it.

"Congratulations, you made them heavier," Chien sassed.

"And distributed that weight so you're not carrying all of it in one place. Trust me on this, it'll work better."

"Oh, I do, but I'm still going to joke about it."

The attendant who'd brought me the supplies watched intently as we tried them on and loaded them up, blinking at the way I didn't struggle with the much heavier load than expected. She ran off afterward like she was looking for someone.

"You're doing it again," Isha quipped, poking me in the arm.

"The words you're looking for are 'Thank you,' my love," I replied. No respect today, none at all.

"For attracting more attention to us."

Shortly thereafter, the attendant and a man I recognized from Rolan's throne room reappeared. The latter came up to us.

"That's an interesting design," he said. "May I?"

When I nodded, he picked up my pack, weighing it, then put it on, moving for a few moments.

"Thoughts?" I asked.

"I see why our master likes you, Justin. I hope you don't mind if I make more of these."

"Go ahead."

"I'm Lein, by the way, one of those responsible for bringing new things to pass around here. As a thanks, would you mind if I showed you one of my own creations? I think it will make the beginning of your journey easier at least."

There were enthusiastic nods from our group. I was excited to meet another inventor, another man I could discuss things with.

"When you're ready to leave then," he said, seeming happy to wait.

It didn't take us long, and soon we were escorted just outside. A short walk away was Lien's invention, hidden away under a branch with a little platform leading out to it. I looked up, seeing the spool and the person working it and understood immediately.

"With this we can speed our way back to the bottom. It doesn't go all the way, but there are several more on the way, and with them we can bypass most of the walking. Though a lot of people don't like them."

It was a lift, but more like a basic crane than anything else.

"I can't believe we had to walk all that way," Chien sighed.

"Most people don't like them," Lien said with a shake of his head.

"Because it's incredibly dangerous," I mumbled. Using this for people was insane.

"Would you like to try it out? You'll get back to the more traveled branches in no time at all."

"Yes," Isha answered for us, stepping on.

"Wait," I tried.

"I do not want to walk that far," she said. "If something happens, can you fix it?"

I did some quick calculations based on how much magic I had left. If things did go south I could at least keep us below bone-breaking velocities and guide us somewhere safe to land.

"Yes . . ."

"Then get on, Elian. Taking hours of marching off our journey is a gift."

Hesitantly, I did. Looking down, I white-knuckled one of the ropes holding the thing together. Lien, who I'd thought I might like, seemed totally at peace with riding the death trap down. There weren't even handrails, for goodness sake, just an open platform with a rope lowering it. For cargo that might be fine, but it was stressing me out.

"You good?" Chien inquired, seeing how tense I was.

"One day, Chien, I'm going to make a proper elevator, with magnetic locks, and safety cables, and a frame, and a box, and inspections, so many inspections," I said through gritted teeth.

"What do you mean?" the 'inventor' asked.

"Don't ask that; you'll just get nonsense answers," Isha said, patting him on the shoulder. "Well, nonsense until he builds it and shows you what he means."

"I'd still like to know," he said, turning to me.

"There are so many problems with this."

I went on to ask him questions about what would happen if the line broke, or if we were blown off course by wind, or knocked off because there was nothing keeping us on this thing. He didn't seem too concerned about my questions until I went into detail about how that rope would fatigue over time, how it would break, and not *if*, but *when* and *how* people would die, without question. He looked concerned by the time we made it to the first landing and led us to the next "lift" of his. On that ride down, I went into detail about how there should be safety measures—not one, not two, but plans upon plans for failure. How we should remain safe so long as the world kept working, as it did regardless of what happened. There was so much that for the next two or three lifts I berated him about potential dangers and how these things should only be used for cargo.

"But you're still riding it?" he asked.

"I have enough power to catch us all if something fails. If I can't, Chien should be able to at least keep us from dying from the fall." My companions at least seemed relieved by that.

"Ah, I see. Well, that was the last one anyway." It shaved off several hours of walking down, down, down. The fact that we didn't have to basically circle the tree over and over really had shortened the journey, even if it had stressed me.

"Thank you," I said finally, and we began our walk.

"Going back up, Lien?" one of the operators asked as we turned to leave.

"I, uh, I think I'll walk actually," he said quietly. It gratified me that at least he was learning.

Isha briefly pinched my ear. "Poor guy," she said. "You ruined his dream."

"Kept him from killing himself," I retorted, poking her. Poking her was fun any time, even if she slapped my hand away.

"Well, it was fun at least," Chien said as we walked toward the path that would lead us out of the city. With our memories, even seeing it once was enough for us to know the way.

It was sad that we'd lost Rolan from this trip, but he'd be here when we got back. Maybe I would come to see him some time, come and show him some of the things I made, and how he could as well, to improve his people's lives. He was a good enough guy that I didn't think he'd abuse the privilege too badly.

CHAPTER 14

OUT OF THE FOREST
AND INTO THE TREES

The trail out of Rolan's lands was sedate. We walked along the paths through the trees, taking our time as we picked our way to the northwest. With the supplies we had and the time we'd taken, there was no shortage or rush.

Isha still stopped to trade with a few of the roaming merchants we met. I had a feeling that there were either more of them here, or there were so many fewer paths that we were meeting more of them. Those seemed the most likely explanations, at least, as nobody really walked along the ground in the forest. It meant that though there weren't really fewer people, they seemed more concentrated, and we passed basically every village regardless of if we wanted to or not.

Nobody stopped us on our way out, either, at least not more than just to talk. A lot of the elders were curious where exactly we thought we were going, but when it was explained they let us pass. After all, we'd seen their ancient already, and he'd not thrown us off his tree—something I later learned was an occasional execution method—so we must be fine.

The village structure was similar to ours, and that made sense. One older elf was leading the others and was younger than the rest. Even in the trees there must still be monsters now and then, and a more powerful individual would be needed to fight them. Their gathering was far, far different though. These elves didn't do as much digging for roots as our people did, instead preferring vines, ferns, flowers, nuts, and mosses that could be harvested from their treetop homes or grown there.

They even had a basic form of something I was stoked to see.

"Look on the roofs, Chien," I said as we passed through one village.

"Looks like moss," he answered, squinting.

"The same moss they gave us to eat," Isha said, seeing where I was going with this.

"Yes, they're growing it here themselves. Even if it can't be gathered, this will make it a sustainable food!" I was so proud of them.

"Is this that agriculture stuff you're going on about again? It looks nothing like what you did back in Elayatol," Isha griped.

"Of course not," I replied. "That was a ground-based attempt."

"That made a mess."

"And here they're growing it up in the trees. This is also a perfect environment for moss, warm and wet."

My lover rolled her eyes. She'd never thought much of my attempts at farming. The first had been when I was much smaller, back in the village we both grew up in. It was an abject failure, not just because I wasn't a farmer, but because nobody cared. The food there had been too common, too easy to gather, so nobody saw any point to it.

I'd had some success in Atal, selling the concept to people who were in discord about gathering rights. That was all, though, and I'd even explained it to the ruler of the city once. He'd understood it, and what it would do, but saw no point to it either. After all, the population didn't grow much or fast, and gatherers could get plenty for the city without any of the hard work farming would take. Perhaps he'd been right. With how many people died before getting too old, maybe farming wasn't needed yet. I'd like to change that at some point, though.

After weeks of travel the trees got smaller and smaller, and they also changed type. The large ones of the forest looked more like deciduous trees, but as we moved north there were smaller trees interspersed, with needles rather than leaves. There were few at first, just a couple here and there tossed throughout their mighty cousins, but soon the larger ones shrank and were replaced.

Eventually, the bridges couldn't keep us so high, the giants being too far apart, and sadly we made our way back down to the ground. As we did, we got one look outward over the branches and in the direction we were going. I saw the sheer rock faces before us and cringed.

At first I thought they were mountains because that would have at least made a lick of sense, but no, not mountains—a plateau, a very sizable one. I couldn't see either end, as what seemed to be a sheer face rose from the ground, reaching upward to the heavens. We even managed to get a nice cold breeze as we stood there looking at it.

"Why does everyone have to live up high?" Chien asked, looking at the direction we were going.

"Better question—why did nobody tell us what exactly we were going into?" Isha retorted.

"Because they like laughing at people," I told both of them. "I know for a fact that Rolan is sitting back there rolling and smacking his throne at the idea of us marching through what is definitely going to be a blizzard. And if you think Jina isn't the kind of person who'd let us go into this unprepared, you're wrong. She's basically a sadist."

"Jerk," Chien said, shaking his head.

"Nah, he didn't warn us, but at least he gave us winter gear. Even if he had warned us, it wouldn't have changed anything. We knew it was going to be cooler, but not this much." I was pretty sure I could see ice decorating the top of that thing, the light white-blue color distinctive even at this distance.

"Okay, how are we getting up that, though? It looks perfectly flat." Isha didn't seem pleased.

"Don't know yet, but I'd wager there are crevices we can use. May also be time to develop a flight spell." While thinking about how to do that, I descended the bridge to the ground.

"Wonder why they don't bring the big trees all the way in," Chien asked as we walked forward, the number of pines steadily growing.

"May not be able to," I said. "That plateau is rock; no doubt about it. Soil might have something similar below us, getting really shallow really fast." A lot of the depictions of the ocean were like that back on Earth, with a hard falloff in depth at a certain point. It would at least explain the change in vegetation.

Over the next few days we found ourselves not in our normal forest but in something I recognized from my previous home in the Carolinas, a pine forest. It was pines, pines, pines everywhere, needles everywhere, slippery but at least soft. There were signs of previous burns, but as we approached the rainy season, none of those were currently active. By some miracle we'd also missed the pollen season. If we'd arrived to clouds of yellow dust, which must surely arrive yearly, I might have just turned around and waited, or burned it down. My eyes found the little orange indicators that it was soon to come though, currently shining a brilliant yellowish-green.

Everything not covered in needles or the few shrubs trying to make it through the acidic soil was sand, foot deep and loose. At least there were no monsters, which gave me plenty of time to have flashbacks to my first youth and all the national parks I'd been drug through by well-meaning teachers and parents.

CHAPTER 15

YELLOW TIDE

The base of the rise wasn't quite sheer, but it was near enough to appear that way. All around the base were stones, starting slowly at first but quickly piling up from where they'd fallen from above. After a couple hundred feet, though, it went back to being a pine forest, clearly marking the barrier between the two regions.

"Well, that doesn't look climbable," Chien pointed out.

"Not easily at least," I agreed.

We'd managed to spot a waterfall as we got closer. I had questions like where the water was coming from and all manner of other things, but those could wait. Right now we needed to figure out how to ascend this thing, and it didn't appear to want to cooperate.

The water crashed down, hitting a few spots that might have been capable of holding us, but it was probably slick. Most of the water was, of course, being turned into mist before it hit the ground, forming a sort of cloud, but there was a small lake at the base of it all, before continuing on in a little stream.

"Those rocks look odd, like they don't belong," Isha said, pointing at a line of stones, each about the height of one of us. I had to agree. They were off; their color was different.

"Let's see where they go then; maybe we weren't the first ones here," I said with a shrug. It was better than any of the other ideas I currently had.

The stones meandered up to the side of the waterfall and then slowly made their way behind it, revealing a small cave, and hidden within the mist were steep stairs. Things like this weren't common, but neither were they unheard of. Elves lived long lives, and those who traveled often had the power to change the landscape. Even if they didn't feel like leaving large signs, they might want a way to come back and forth. The hidden safe house was wet, but with some effort one could make a fire and take shelter from wind or night, and the stairs would lead the way up. These could be hundreds or even thousands of years old.

Of course, this little spot was a natural place for a rest. It was visible, so anyone trying to travel this route would have no issues finding it, and it had plenty of water for washing or drinking. Food would be sparse, as the pool had little other than tiny fish and some plants, but that wasn't a big a deal in the grand scheme of things.

Chien checked the cave while I made my way to the stairs. The craftsmanship was unimpressive. They were uneven, oddly shaped, and tall, but they would do. Interestingly, someone had taken the time to score the surfaces deeply, meaning that at least traction wouldn't be an issue.

"Find anything?" I asked as he returned.

"Whoever used it hasn't been here in a while. There was a barrier a few steps in to keep animals out, and you can see where the fire pit is, but beyond that there's nothing of note. Doubt anyone leaves things in there."

"Stairs are rough. I'm betting they just let the rock break where it would," I mused, running my hand over one. "Let's stay the night, and in the morning we'll head up."

"Achoo!" came a small sneeze behind me, and I saw Isha rubbing her nose. "Good, something about this place is bugging me," she said.

The next morning we slowly cleaned up our camp. There was no great hurry, so we slept in—finally having a sheltered spot in which to do so. Even the noise from the waterfall was peaceful—repetitive and calming as it splashed into the pool.

"I'm going to go wash," Isha declared the next morning. "Who knows when we'll get another chance." She had a point.

I gave her a smile, and she flicked my ear before turning to leave. Perhaps in a bit I could join her . . .

Before I got the camp fully ready she came back, dripping wet and having clearly hurried to get her clothes on. Chien and I were still going through some of our things, repacking and readying for the ascent.

"Justin, something's happening," she said, slightly alarmed.

We followed her outside to see what she was talking about. The wind. Everywhere the wind was tainted, stained with the yellow I'd so feared just a day or two ago. It was late enough that the forest had dried from the dew, and now that the wind was picking up it was releasing its sneeze-inducing load everywhere.

"What is that?" Chien asked, having never experienced pines before.

"A headache; we need to climb."

Our female companion was already beginning to sneeze, making cute little noises as her nose tried to rid itself of the invaders. I, too, could feel it coming on and had no desire to be here when it arrived in full force, so we quickly gathered up our supplies and began the ascent.

Chien was leading, while I brought up the rear, making sure Isha didn't slip during her intermittent sneezing fits. Both Chien and I had stayed at the cave, protected by the falling mist from the allergen while she'd gone right into the brewing storm. Her desire to be clean driving her right into the itching, snot-producing clouds.

An hour or two in, and we found a spot to rest. A little place where a section of the plateau had shorn away, leaving a flat spot on the cliff. The stairs we were using were nearly hidden, hard to make out on the rock from the ground, particularly against the plain backdrop. The climb was, in one word, awful. My legs were burning from the odd, uneven movements, and my companions looked much the same.

Below us, though, the clouds of pollen roiled in the breeze, the haze drifting along between trees in the circle of life. It looked almost like smog, or fog, rolling over the landscape, save for the color.

"Is that stuff dangerous?" Chien asked.

"Just makes your face stuffy and gross," I informed him, pointing to Isha, who was currently undergoing the symptoms. She must have been particularly sensitive to it.

"What is it?" she asked, having never seen pollen like this before.

"You know how when you're with someone and they . . . you know, and it's a mess?" She looked at me like I was asking stupid questions. Certainly she knew. We did that all the time. "It's like that, for trees."

"I breathed in tree goop?" she asked. Interestingly, in our tongue, semen was not always addressed as "seed" as it was in English. Instead, most of the more impolite words focused on the consistency.

"Basically."

I heard Chien begin to cackle and realized too late that I really should have held that explanation back. Her eyes darkened a bit. "We will never speak of this again," she informed us.

"Haha, feeling unhappy Isha?" Chien teased.

"You know we were all in that, right Chien? Everyone got a dose, even if Isha got the worst of it."

That put a damper on his mood, something our female member took advantage of.

"What Chien? Don't want to imagine yourself covered in tree goop?" she asked, smiling.

"And here I thought we weren't talking about this again," he grumbled, before standing and making for the next set of stairs.

"Oh? Are you sure? I don't think I mind nearly as much as you seem to."

Exercising all of my composure, I stayed out of it. Pollen didn't bother me much. Back in my first life, this was a regular occurrence.

CHAPTER 16

GLACIAL

"I'd like to ask that the next place we go, we avoid climbs," Chien said as we neared the top of the cliff.

"I agree," Isha added.

"Yes, yes, nobody likes trying to make it up a mountain, or a giant tree, or whatever, and we all agree it sucks." I really didn't want to have massive climbs, but it seemed as if that was just the way my life was going right now.

Our ascent had been slow, mind-numbingly slow. That wasn't to say that we weren't making progress. We were, but with this particular steep climb, it was just taking much longer. It was also getting cooler as we rose, away from the warmth that we were used to and into something quite different. By evening, we had all pulled out the extra clothing Rolan had given us, trying to get just a little warmer.

The next day we made it to where the ice began, and I could see that we'd be upon a deep sheet of ice soon. Perhaps there were parts that wouldn't be covered by it, but some decidedly would be. We also met one of our worst obstacles yet—the ice moved, not quickly, not much, but it moved, enough that there were no stairs in it. It looked like parts broke off, falling to the ground far below, and carrying with them bits of the glacier.

"How are we supposed to get up? Melt new steps?" Chien asked.

"That would take days. You two have been practicing your ability to move things right?" When they both nodded, I continued. "I'll do the bulk of it, but help me push us upward. It looks to only be a couple hundred feet."

"Flight is supposed to be really hard, boss," Chien pointed out.

"If not for this, I wouldn't try, but we can do it."

They got close, joining me in a big hug, and I began to wrap us in a shell of my magic. It had been some time since I'd used so much of my power, but it still came to my bidding without delay, forming and molding around us, just as I'd imagined. It was like taking a burden upon my back, but not too difficult.

As I began to lift us, I understood Chien's statements. Picking yourself up like this took a lot of magic, quite a lot indeed, and if I hadn't been practicing controlling kinetic force in such large quantities in the city, I doubted I'd be able to pull us all up. It was also disorienting; the sensation was odd, making it hard to stabilize us. I suspected it had something to do with the fact that I was moving as I tried to move myself, making the whole thing shift perspective around me quite a bit.

Added to those complications was the fact that this wasn't a brute force type of spell. No, I needed to lift without crushing, and pay attention to orientation. Small movements due to wind had to be compensated for too, and without a stable base that got more and more awkward.

Isha didn't seem too bothered, but Chien looked positively green by the time we reached the lip of the glacier, a small push depositing us a few feet from the edge.

"There's got to be a better way to do that," I declared, sinking down to take a break.

"I feel like someone's picked me up and spun me around their head," my assistant agreed.

"Babies," Isha teased. "It wasn't that bad." Chien and I glared at her, and she just smiled.

We stood up, brushing off her comments and looked around. Behind us the green carpet of the forest stretched out into the distance, the foliage seeming small from where we stood. Before us, brilliant white was swept clean in a few places to reveal the deep azure ice beneath. A few places also had spits of black rock protruding from them, places where there'd been peaks or rises that for whatever reason resisted the encroaching ice.

"You're sure people live up here?" Isha asked.

"Supposedly."

"How?"

"No idea, but we need to find them."

All of us were cold, but after some brief discussion about techniques we wrapped ourselves in warm air, cushions to block the chill wind and protect our own heat as we moved forward. To my surprise, we soon found that the landscape wasn't quite as empty as it had appeared. As we approached one of the rocks, I could make out small plants, darker than I was used to, but present and nestled around the base and in the crevices, looking for any form of nutrient. There were also a few places in the snowy areas that looked like they had some tracks, but it was impossible for me to tell how old they were.

Before it got too late we began searching for a place to rest. In the forests we could whip something up in a hurry, but here? I was unsure, but perhaps something built from ice or snow would be best if we couldn't find a cave. We'd also have to prepare it right, or we'd be miserably cold, and in potential danger.

Luck wasn't on our side on the cave front, but ice was everywhere, and between Chien and I we could carve blocks of it with relative ease. Large square chunks of the glacial material were easy to come by and move into place, and with effort we built a little hut that looked like a mixture between an igloo and something one would find in a block-based video game.

"Sleeping on ice is insane," Isha grumbled.

"Who's being a baby now?" I asked, shifting some ice into place that served as the roof.

"Ice is cold, Elian," she said, reverting to my old name again. She was about the only one who switched between them these days, and only when she was truly frustrated.

"We'll sleep on the furs," I told her. "It will be fine. Haven't you learned to trust me by now?"

She just pouted, but when the makeshift hut was complete, she joined me in what was going to be my bed. That might have been a very generous term, but at least it was a divot where I could pile up any covering we had to try and keep warm.

"I'm not going to be cold tonight," she declared, ignoring the spot I'd made for her. She buried herself in my spot, looking at me expectantly.

"You said keeping the air close was a good idea, right? Maybe we should build little chambers around our beds too." Chien properly read the room and brought us in some ice for just that purpose, and it was a good thing he did.

I was glad for my assistant, for privacy had been hard to come by, and Isha's actions weren't entirely for the purpose of warmth. Over the past few weeks, the three of us had spent most of our time together, and within earshot, but with so much building material around, more individualized rooms were now quite possible.

CHAPTER 17

POCKETS OF LIFE

The plateau's winter seemed perpetual, snow and ice never going away. Rather than rain, we had snow, destroying visibility and blowing against us hour after hour. Days passed as what would have been the rainy season advanced, and we found ourselves practically buried every morning.

That wasn't to say we didn't make any progress inland, for we certainly did, nor that we didn't find anything at all, for that too would be untrue. The first came when I was digging us out of our nightly shelter one morning.

I could have been digging with hands, or perhaps one of the few tools I'd brought along, but no, magic made things easier, and there was no reason for me to waste time and effort trying to do with physical work what I could more easily do with nothing other than the power of my mind. When all of a sudden a head popped out of the side of the tunnel.

It was a rabbit, a bit large perhaps, and pure white and surprised to have met me here. For a moment the two of us blinked at each other, eyes locked before it panicked and turned, fleeing back into its tunnel. I was so surprised that I didn't even try to catch it. We could have used the meat, sure, but it wasn't dire or anything, and I took it as a sign of good luck. This showed me that there was still some life up here, even if most of it was hidden.

Leaving the foot on the lucky rabbit worked, as by midday the snow had all but ceased. That was good, as I was getting tired of keeping all of the spells needed to manage the cold flakes at bay. As the winds slowed and flakes stopped drifting down in waves, a patch of small trees was revealed a few hundred feet away. The little evergreens struggled, but they pushed their way upward, looking for some freedom from the knee-high snow.

Seeing a chance to make our journey easier, we pulled some of the ones that looked to be doing poorly. After all, wood was not exactly common here, and we wouldn't want to deprive the locals of prime materials. The bits we took were spindly and whiplike and made the perfect base for a rudimentary sled. Sled building had been one of the first things I'd taught Chien, and while these were certainly different than the sturdier constructions now used in and around Atal, this one would be excellent for snow.

A vehicle, even the poor little one they fashioned, greatly sped up our progress. No more was our group trying to push through all the snow, struggling with each step or melting our way forward with magic. Now they sailed across the top of it. Magical pushes and a few good hills made things easier, and even fun at times.

That's not to say there were no hiccups. Several times they capsized, sending their whole crew sprawling to the sides and causing no small amount of bruises. Even sore, their speed and sheer enjoy-ment made it all worth it.

"Where are we going anyway?" Chien asked as they took a break for lunch.

"No idea," I admitted honestly, getting sour looks from him and Isha.

"Seriously?" he asked.

"Yeah, I don't know my way around here. My best idea is to wan-der for a while until they spot us and decide to come talk. Do you have any clue where their camp is? Or even how to navigate in this mess? I mean, I can get us in a general direction and whatnot, but there have to be paths and passes somewhere."

"So, what's our general direction then?" Isha didn't seem impressed with my plan.

"East, with a bit of a north or south lean at any given time, depending on what we see. If you see anything you want to check out, we can."

An hour later, Isha was the one to point a place out. It looked to be a dip in the horizon surrounded by small hills. Seemed to me a good a place as any to check out, and if not, we could make camp there tonight, as it should at the very least be nicely sheltered.

We weren't the only ones interested, it appeared, as a small herd of some kind of deer had taken up residence at the bottom. There were less than twelve, but all of the bucks had horns that glowed slightly, surrounding a small orb in their heads.

"Take them?" Chien asked.

"Magic, definitely magic. Let's watch and see what we can learn before we try anything. I don't fancy fighting some kind of powerful beast if we don't have to."

While the animals seemed agitated by our presence, occasionally looking up where we waited on the edge of the little bowl, the fact that nobody was getting any closer or displaying more than interest seemed to keep them calm. Sadly, that meant that I didn't really learn anything about them, but it was at least a restful way to spend part of my afternoon, or at least it would have been.

"Hey," called a sharp, harsh tone from nearby. "What exactly do you think you're doing? This is our hunt."

I jumped, and we all immediately began to look around for the unknown voice. My two companions looked nervous, but I pushed out a wave of mana, trying to sense anything.

That failed, of course. I'd never tried anything like sonar or the like before, magical or otherwise, and so it was a complete bust. That didn't mean it did nothing, though, and our visitor wouldn't know that.

"Reveal yourself," I said to no one in particular, getting ready to fight.

A small pile of snow, not even ten feet from us rose up to reveal an elf in a full cloth outfit that matched perfectly with the color of the snow, looking like it was one with the surroundings.

"Don't play coy with me. We've been following this herd for days. They're ours. If you want some deer yourself, go find others. I'm not giving up a group I've put this much time and effort into. Also, keep your voice down, you dolt, or you'll scare them all away."

"I don't want the deer," I told the white-clad hunter. "I'm a messenger sent to speak to the locals." He looked at me like I was an idiot. "It's true," I continued. "I really am looking to spread news."

"Whatever," he replied. "You can wait here then, and when we're done, I'll take you to see someone, but we need those antlers for our home."

"Fine, like I said, I don't care about the deer."

"Then you're an idiot. They're needed, particularly for our house. We're always trying to get just enough."

CHAPTER 18

ICEHOME

I stood back and watched the locals go to work. This valley had to have been prepared; either that or they knew the deer would come here because this was where they were going to take them. I didn't see them at first, but when it all started, dozens of people seemed to pop out of the landscape, spells and spears hurling toward the surprised animals.

They'd formed a loose circle around the herd, and it looked like they were keen on keeping each and every one of the animals from escaping. I wondered briefly what they wanted the antlers for but soon decided that it probably didn't matter too much to me. Perhaps they needed them for weapons or some form of magical ink like those in the tattoos I'd learned to make. Regardless, that wasn't what I was here for.

One of the deer jumped, making it over their line and charging for the lip of the valley near where we were. It seemed that our new companion was supposed to be part of the attackers, but in coming up here to deal with us, he'd left a small hole in the force. I heard him curse behind me, but since I wanted his help, I figured I could do something about it.

The animal turned as it neared us, clearly trying to get away, and that was the moment I fanned a flurry of kinetic bolts at it. The thing was fast, and I didn't want to let it get away. I was at least careful to make sure the locals weren't in my line of fire and that I wouldn't hit the antlers even by mistake; no need to antagonize anyone.

The newcomer looked at me warily as the creature went down spasming. Of course I'd not even raised a hand to shoot that volley, and it was clearly something that only someone who had real power could do.

"That kill is ours," he complained, though I could tell he didn't want to fight me on his own.

"I already agreed to that. It was merely an act of goodwill since you seem to want them so badly."

Chien was chuckling behind me. Now that we could see the elves below us, we were getting a measure of their abilities. Between the two of us, we probably could have driven this group off had we wanted to, and that wasn't even including Isha. She wasn't as suited for combat as we were, but her scream attack wasn't something to underestimate, and against those without enough magic to defend against it would cause havoc. Cleanup soon began, and it was quick and dirty. Mostly they just drained the blood from the kills and opened them to remove the organs. All of this was, of course, packed into skins and containers that each of the hunters had on them, and all of this was done with hurried moves.

As they did so, I took my time to examine their clothes. Each seemed to be made from sewn-together skins, but rather than leave the outsides as they were, there was snow worked in. Each of them had a layer of the white fluffy stuff all over them, further adding to the illusion. It was also some of the best craftsmanship I'd seen from my fellow elves, if I were being honest.

"So, is there a village nearby?" Chien asked while I looked over the progress they were making on the deer.

"Village? The Icehome is a few days away by foot. How do you not know this?"

"This is our first time here," I interjected. "Did I not already explain this? We are looking for your ancient to deliver our message."

"Hmm, very well, but know that all who stay must contribute to keeping our home warm."

I wasn't sure what he meant by that, so I shrugged. "We'll do what we can within reason."

The hunters packed the animals on their backs, distributing the load. It wasn't lost on me that a few were eyeing our little sled, watching it move across the snow effortlessly. They too had some manner of not sinking, though that was in the form of huge furry shoes that kept them from sinking. None of them asked to use the sled or said anything at all really.

While our newly met traveling buddies did their best to ignore us, we made good time. It was only a few nights more of travel before we reached our destination. They, of course, had their own manner of tent, which they could deploy with some effort. For our part, though, we kept using the igloo technique, something which drew some interest. Perhaps they could have used something similar, but oddly, there were no magic users among them, only elves with basic abilities like all members of our race seemed to develop.

When we arrived, I agreed that Icehome was a fitting name for this location. The place was a glacier, a massive wall of ice with a large arch carved into one side. From here it was impossible to tell just how big the place was, but looking at the sheet of ice they'd picked to build on, it could be of conceivably massive proportions, rivaling Atal or the trees of the forest-dwelling elves with ease.

We walked in without any opposition, though. Since we were with a known group, that probably helped. As soon as we were inside the doors, really large slabs of stone were moved into place, and another elf approached us. I could tell by the shock of white hair on one side of his head that he was older, and he looked curious.

"Welcome, outsider," he said. "I am Lorn, and I keep this area for Matriarch Neera." I had to guess, but perhaps Icehome was divided up into regions or something? Regardless, it didn't change what I needed to do.

"Greetings, I've come with a message for your eldest. Am I right that this would be the Matriarch?" I asked.

"Yes. You may stay while awaiting an audience, but know that all must contribute to keeping our home warm."

I nodded, having already learned that much from one of the hunters. "So long as it is not odious, I agree."

"Oh, it's nothing horrid, I assure you," he said with a smile.

Admittedly, Icehome, despite the name, was quite warm inside. I wondered how they were managing that but knew that patience would save me the trouble in time. The elder excused himself to deal with the incoming hunters, and while he did that, Isha tugged lightly on my arm.

"Look at them; they're so pale," she whispered, seeming to find it strange.

It was true. I hadn't noticed because I was sort of used to differing skin tones in my previous life, but as they stripped off their coats and protections it became clear that they were different from us. All of the elves I'd met had been slightly darker in tone. It didn't really match anything from Earth, but was closest perhaps to southern European or perhaps someone from the tropics. However, the elves of Icehome were paper white. Their features were much like ours, and like us their eyes came in a few differing colors, but they looked so different. They really must have been isolated for that to happen.

Lorn returned shortly thereafter, looking pleased. "I've sent your request for a meeting to the Matriarch. Shall I show you where you may stay until she's ready to meet with you?"

"Please do. How long does it normally take to arrange such a meeting?" I asked.

"It will take as long as it takes," he answered, and I had a feeling that she would be in no hurry at all.

CHAPTER 19

HEATING ROOM

I still can't believe that's how they're doing it," I complained, and not for the first time.

"Is he still going on?" Chien asked as he joined us in the little common room between our sleeping arrangements.

"Yes, and refuses to hear otherwise," Isha said, giggling.

"I refuse to hear otherwise because this is the most asinine, most senseless, most . . . inefficient way to heat something I may have ever seen." They both just sighed and began to tune me out again.

Icehome was a lovely structure and extended deep into the underlying stone. That was important, as it meant that there was always going to be some residual warmth. Once underground, the temperature just didn't change that much. While they all lived down below, the offices and official areas were above, inside the glacier.

My issue was that while they knew they needed to keep it warm, and were even devoting time to such an operation, they were doing it so poorly. Fires underground like this wouldn't have been practical, but boilers, or some kind of local heaters, would have worked. Of course, that wasn't what they'd gone with at all.

"Well, you're up." Chien said. "Feel free to complain to our hosts."

"I may," I retorted.

With a sigh, I turned and left our quarters, passing by several lamps in the hall. These were fashioned from the antlers of the deer we'd seen before, shaped and used to keep this place bright since there was no sun down here. Luckily, the "heating room" wasn't far from where we stayed, something granted to us by our hosts after they discovered we all had proper magic.

After going down several sets of stairs, I found the temperature ticking up perceptibly until I finally found my way into the central area of the whole city-like hive of the northern elves. The room itself was swelteringly hot, and I had to stop at one of the little alcoves to remove most of my clothing. This wasn't odd, as almost all of the elves in here were either in very little, or, in a few cases, nothing at all.

The room itself was the size of a small stadium and divided into tiers, each moving downward until they got to the very center, where there stood a large crimson crystal. Each successive tier was nicer and nicer, with water features and baths for cooling, and even food and drinks brought to those resting on the tier if you were low enough.

It was a hive of activity, particularly the upper levels. People were coming in, focusing for a few moments, and then leaving. All of this was enforced by a handful of guards who were watching what everyone was doing. The elves up here had developed a few unique techniques for just this place, ones they were more than happy to teach us.

"Welcome back, Justin. Heading down to the fourth?" asked one of the guards as I left the alcove.

"Yes," I said as I spun up the first of the tricks they'd taught us, a sort of rope to feed mana into the central crystal at a distance. I knew the expectations for each tier, and set it appropriately.

"Goodness, friend, you know you could get to the third with ease, right? I can see your aura. Maybe if you really tried, you could be on the second, though, not for long." The guard did as all the others and pushed for more effort, more mana.

"No thank you," I said. "I really am just here for a time until I can meet with the leadership." I always gave the same response.

The guard didn't continue to argue. He only smiled as I picked my way down the tiers. Some of those on the top frowned at me, but they weren't here for more than a few moments, just enough time to dump their mana into the stone and leave. They were the workers, the lowest class of this place, with each successive step closer getting more wealthy, more important.

Heating in Icehome was done through a form of passive ventilation. Cold air was brought in through a series of tunnels, pumped into this room through grates beneath the crystal and rose through holes in the ceiling to heat the rooms above. There was no insulation, no closing off of unused sections, no shutoffs or the like, just a rising of air to circulate through the whole hive, for Icehome could hardly be described as anything else.

I passed hundreds of elves as I descended. Icehome contained thousands upon thousands, even if relatively few were here currently. Soon enough, I found a spot that I favored for these required jaunts, a little area on the fourth tier where there was a small pool to cool off and a few pleasant benches. Cooling off was a requirement as you got closer to the crystal, as even at this distance, it felt like I was standing near my forge.

Each tier down the people changed too. I'd thought that the hunters we met were pale, but they were nothing compared to those here. Spellcasters were treasured, and in this society they spent all of their time warming the compound or relaxing away from the cold. By the fifth tier, people looked like paper, and when the closest in passed by, you could practically see their veins through their skin.

"Ah, welcome back, Justin," one of the local women purred as I entered the water. She got close, but not too close, knowing I wasn't interested.

"Hello again, Imra," I replied cordially.

"I thought you might come back when Chien left. He is a cutie, isn't he?" Chien was fawned over, mostly because he had power and was clearly single.

"He's a good kid."

Soon I laid back. Feeding magic into the crystal wasn't particularly arduous, but it was boring, so I began to play with a small bit of water, snapping it into rings and various shapes as a sort of fidgeting.

"Hey, you're pretty good at that," one of the others observed, coming to see what I was doing. I saw him look on in interest as I ran the little trickle of fluid through geometric shapes and symbols.

As the other elf tried to repeat my actions I watched, frowning. This was the thing I hated most; they were all bad at magic. He frowned, eyes furrowing in concentration as he tried to get the spell to form properly, and if I was to judge, using far too much mana to do it. All of the casters here spent so much time pushing their mana into this damn crystal to improve their social standing that almost none of them actually practiced with their magic.

"It should be effortless—control, shape, and continue," I instructed, signaling Imra and a few others to come closer.

"Effortless? For someone in the second tier maybe," he complained, unable to even get a handful of water to shape into a proper clean ring.

"No, you do not need more mana; you need control of the mana," I said, using my term for the magical energy even if they called it something else.

"Where did you learn?" one of the nearby girls asked with a smile.

I sighed. "Where I'm from, when a child is found to have magic they are pulled away from the others and instructed by an elder until they can safely control it. You can spend days or weeks alone doing little more than practicing until you get at least the basics. Do they not do something similar here?"

"No," Imra answered. "When you're found to have power you're brought here and taught to donate it until you're tired. Then you know what tier you're in and get better rooms, better food, and all that. Because you're happy and tired, you never cause problems."

There was a deep desire to punch whoever came up with that system burning in my heart. Sure, it meant that the kids were safe to be around, but it also hamstrung them from ever getting stronger. The whole thing was bread and circuses as far as I was concerned. Well, since the esteemed Matriarch Neera didn't seem bothered to see me, I'd see what I could do about getting her attention.

"Well, if anyone wants, I could run through a few basic exercises to improve your magic. I'm pretty sure they even improve your overall amount of mana over time, so . . ." Several jumped at the opportunity, and I smiled. The simple things I could teach them would make them all the more able to oppose those in power should they ever decide to be a thorn in someone's side.

CHAPTER 20

STIRRING THE POT

I spent the better part of several hours giving short lessons in magic to the elves of Icehome. There were issues, of course, mostly that I had to limit what I was teaching to the absolute smallest things. They didn't want to "waste" their mana on my teachings when it could cause issues for them or their families; so many only wanted tiny tricks.

That wasn't too much of a problem, though, as there were tons of things I could do with only the tiniest trickle of power. Most of these were parlor tricks, like small color-changing lights, sparks, illusions, and most popular, the manipulation of water from the cooling pools. Eventually, a few of the watchers in this room came to see why so many were gathered around, but since there was no disturbance in the flow of energy to their precious crystal, they didn't complain.

"You're pretty good at this," Imra observed as we wound down for the day. "You know, you could probably go with the stronger hunters to get a personal fire crystal if you wanted. My cousin did years ago, and the matriarch was so thrilled she met with him personally."

"My own personal fire crystal?" I asked the flirt. "Like the one in here?"

"Well, sort of," she said. "They're normally only the size of a grain of sand or something, and kept in sap or little stone boxes. My cousin keeps his in his rooms to keep them warm himself. Said it was a lot easier than coming to donate here, and works better too." Of course it worked better. It wasn't trying to heat an entire fucking mountain of stone.

"Interesting, so people want those?" I asked innocently.

"Oh yes, though they only come from large beasts in the south. It's said there's this large hill of rock that spits fire, and the monsters there have little tiny ones in their bodies. You need to use magic to find them, though. Supposedly it's where the matriarch got the one for Icehome, though she beat a much more fearsome monster than most of our warriors could even consider fighting."

"So, if I could get one . . ." I was already aware of how to make similar things. Heck, my hammer had been an amalgamation of them.

"If you got one, you could have almost anything you wanted for it," she said, smiling like a Cheshire cat.

"Like a meeting with the matriarch."

"You're no fun, you know that?"

"I've been told, but thank you."

I left her then to gather Chien and find Lorn. He might have been in charge of the entry to the hive called Icehome, but as one of the leaders here, I was sure that he could help me with a few small things.

"I cannot help speed the meeting on any more Justin," he said before I even had the chance to speak. "Please stop asking." He was near the main entrance to Icehome, overseeing people coming in and out.

"I'm not here to request that," I told him honestly, though I may have pestered him a few times over the last several days.

"Oh? What do you need then?" the elder asked, clearly disbelieving me.

"A workspace, somewhere plain with stone walls. The main issue is that it's going to get very hot in there and I might damage the rock, so I didn't want to do it in our sleeping area."

"How hot are you going to make it?" he asked, raising an eyebrow.

"Enough to melt stone."

"Why?!"

"Nothing bad, I assure you, but a surprise. Help me with this, and I won't need to pester you about meeting the matriarch again."

He looked at me for a few seconds while solidly tapping his chin. "Your companion Isha, she's done some trading. Don't suppose you'd be willing to trade something?"

Of course Isha was trading; she was always trading for things we needed or things she wanted. She'd gathered several new pelts for bedding and even some lights for when we left this place. In exchange, she'd sold some of the spices and trinkets she'd gotten from Rolan's people. I had no doubt that when we went south she'd trade more.

"Very well, how about this? I'll make you some small gems, they're pretty and I'm sure someone will want them." I could make diamonds almost without effort, so it wasn't like it would be an imposition.

"All right, I can do that."

He handed off some of his duties and led me back down below, all the way to the heating room once more. Here he broke off, making his way all the way down to the center, where he spoke with another elder who joined him coming back up to meet me.

"Lorn says you need a room that you're going to get hot?" she asked.

"Yes, it might damage things." I didn't know this elder, but she seemed to at least consider things.

"All right, I've got somewhere, and the extra heat will be welcome anyway."

People moved quickly out of the small woman's way as she led us around the room, taking me to what looked almost like a storage closet. There were others nearby, but this one was empty. It didn't even have a door, just a small open space in the center. Of course I would have liked some privacy, but it would do.

"Good enough?" she asked.

"It should work. Won't be a problem if I damage the walls, will it?"

"No, I can repair them if needed. Just don't go trying to dig new tunnels or anything."

They left me and I got to work. Was one grain-sized mana crystal enough to get Matriarch Neera's attention? Pfft, I'd constructed a whole hammer made from them, of a different element, granted, but I could do fire. I loved fire, I worked with fire, controlled fire, weaponized fire. Fire and I were friends. By the time I was done, the leader of this conclave would have no choice but to come and see me.

"So, boss, what's the plan?" Chien asked, having kept back while I dealt with the elders.

"First things first." I took a second to grab up a little of the carbon from the air and form some diamonds like I'd promised. I even worked in some of the local stone to give them color, ending up with light yellow crystals.

"You gonna teach me that trick?" he asked.

"Not today," I said. "With that one, I'll need to run you through a lot of things with you, but we're doing a much better trick. Can you put up some barriers for me . . ." I really needed to get around to running him through . . . well a lot of things.

Once we had privacy barriers, I explained how magic crystals were made, and the young man's eyes got wider and wider. It was one of my most closely guarded secrets, but Chien had proven himself time and again, and he deserved to know.

"So, we're going to make one?" he asked.

"One? Oh Chien, who do you think we are? One won't be nearly enough."

CHAPTER 21

BEGINNINGS OF CHAOS

Over the next few days Chien and I worked. Nobody bothered us about heating the hive as a whole, mostly because of the massive quantities of heat being blasted out of the small room we'd taken, and partially because Isha decided to keep up appearances by upping her level of donation to their crystal. She was like that, and I loved her for it, always doing things we never asked for and often not realizing it was sorely needed, never complaining about it; just there, the perfect support for my antics.

For antics was what we were certainly up to. One by one, I began to form crystals from fire magic, encasing each in a tiny gem, just large enough to keep track of the potent magical artifacts. We even ran a few trials, making sure they worked just as well as we thought they would while hidden away in our chambers.

When we finished, we had a total of sixteen: five for each of the members of our group and one additional to kickstart the plan. It had been exhausting. The amount of mana spent had been at the upper limit of what I was capable of. Even with my kinship with fire, the cost was still staggering, much like how it had been when I'd first begun making my hammer.

Chien and I rested with our backs against the outer wall, both dripping sweat and smelling absolutely rancid.

"Just holding that was . . . too much boss. How did you even come up with this?" He'd certainly had his work cut out for him, holding all the heat in he could while I worked.

"Honestly? I just saw one and had a theory. First time I managed it, I passed out."

"I believe that. I can sense the amount of power you're putting forth, you maniac."

We decided to take an extended break, stretching and enjoying a meal. This did not go unnoticed. Soon enough there came a knock at the doorway to our little workroom. Normally there was a small privacy barrier, but we'd dropped it since we weren't talking about anything notable and the work was complete.

"My, my, you two not working? What a change . . ." elder Oma said, voice drifting off as her eyes landed on the back of the room, where a still-glowing section of half-melted rock dug into the wall. "What in the world have you been doing?!" Elder Oma was the small woman who was in charge of this section of Icehome, and the one who'd assigned us this room in the first place. She wasn't as old as my former teacher Jina, but because of her position was one of the more respected people residing here. She'd come by a couple of times to investigate while we were working, but we'd always cleaned up beforehand. Now there was really no need; we were done.

"Making trade goods. What did you think we were doing, elder?" I asked, managing to keep the smile out of my voice.

"Practicing magic, since you seem to enjoy doing so. Wait, what were you making?"

I gave a nod to my apprentice. Since the plan was to start a craze anyway, now was a perfect time. He smiled and nodded acceptance, and I produced the latest of our creations, held tight in a thumb-sized diamond. I always liked diamonds. They were easy, great conductors, and pretty.

She caught the thrown gem with effortless ease, looking deep into it, and her eyebrows began to rise.

"Go ahead and put some of your energy into it," I said. "Give it a try." Her eyes flicked to me as I spoke, and I almost felt the tendril of mana go into the gem before a strong radiating heat filled the area, like we were near a campfire.

"You two look like you have a lot to discuss. Why don't I go see how Isha's doing?" Chien said, quickly excusing himself and slipping away before things got out of hand.

After he'd left, I waited, eyes locked on the older elf as she stood stunned. If she'd been a computer, I would have heard fans spinning right about now as she tried to process the situation. She didn't even move, eyelids just twitching slightly as she kept testing my work.

"You can make a heating crystal?" she almost whispered when she finally managed to speak again. "In just a few days?"

"One? Oh no, I made quite a few. In fact, as my thanks for loaning us this room, why don't you keep that one, Oma? It's the least I can do."

Perhaps I wasn't the nicest person in the world, enjoying the scene as the older elf began to nearly hyperventilate, rubbing one hand along her temple as she tried to work out all the implications of what she'd just been told. I knew these were valuable, treasured items only acquired by those who really, really tried, but perhaps I'd underestimated just how valuable, or how much chaos they might cause. After all, heat was life here in the northern lands of snow and ice, and something as small as this would be a game-changer.

"Ha, ha, ha." Breathless, hysterical laughter was probably not a great sign, or maybe it was an excellent one.

"Why don't you sit down? I was taking a break anyway," I offered, extending my hand to a now open section of the floor.

"Tell me, Justin, what is it you want exactly? What are your goals with these?" she asked after calming down some.

"My goal? Oh, it's very simple," I said. "I'm here to deliver a message to the matriarch; nothing more. I was told that the acquisition of one of these had gotten a man a meeting with her before, so I decided to make a few. Chien will likely go and try to get one, or several, of the more attractive girls around here to give him . . . attentions, for the duration of our stay, if I know him. Isha will trade for goods, and anything she finds interesting." I knew my companions, and a guess told me that was exactly what they would do. Isha loved her trading wherever we went, and Chien was definitely something of a womanizer.

"Haha, so you tired of her games, I see. Though nobody's done something so extreme as this before."

"Quite; why delay us anyway?"

"Our numbers are small in comparison to other groups," she admitted.

"There are a good few here," I disagreed.

"Not in comparison, there aren't." Adding into account all of the villages and the larger cities, she wasn't entirely incorrect. "And we get few visitors. If we can convince even one to stay every few hundred years, it's quite a boon."

"Irritating people isn't a good way to get them to stay," I pointed out.

"It wasn't meant to irritate, rather to give time, time to form relationships, friendships, connections, time for you to like it here, and hopefully decide not to leave. For example, with his power, your apprentice could likely find a mate, and if he did, certainly she wouldn't want him to leave."

"Doubtful from what I know of him, but why?"

"Too much of the same blood is bad. We all know that."

I sighed. She wasn't wrong. Their population was smaller than the other communities, and because of their habits, also weaker, so pushing out and taking a different territory would be rather fraught with danger to the people as a whole. No, trying to keep people around wasn't the worst idea to combat inbreeding; it was just a pain in the neck for me.

"Well, with Chien's proclivities you may well end up with a child or two of different lineage."

That got another laugh from her, and then she looked up more seriously.

"Spreading these around too much will be disruptive, though. Sure, the strong will love them, but those without any power will suffer. They depend on the warmth we generate for their safety and comfort. So, I will ask you not to make any more than you already have."

"Get me a meeting with your matriarch, and I'll be happy to agree."

"Believe me, she will want to speak to you now."

I wasn't sure if that was good or bad, but it was my goal after all.

CHAPTER 22

BOILING OVER

My plan went swimmingly, well, a little too swimmingly. Chien had let Isha know the trading was on while I spoke to the elder, hoping to get attention quickly, and boy had they. She was deep in negotiation with several small clans while he was nowhere to be found by the time I was done.

I'd cleaned myself off before going to join her in her escapades in one of the inner circles of the heating room. Donating mana wasn't a challenge right now for me, and if I were being honest, sitting back in one of the pools while she went back and forth with several other elves was relaxing. I could see why the people here had fallen into the trap they had. It was comfortable.

"We could arrange a whole chamber for you and your family, if you like? I assure you that my brother is the best at making furnishings in all of Icehome, and I know he would be willing," one of the perspective traders offered, trying to get Isha to agree.

"We need portable goods, not large ones," she clarified.

This had been going on for the better part of an hour, with more people appearing with offers slowly over the course of that hour. I watched on from the side, happy to be ignored for the most part. That looked to be changing, though, as Oma and several others with shocks of white hair came up from the inner tiers. I hadn't even seen her return after she'd run off to see the matriarch, so I was surprised.

"Come to stop things, Elder Oma?" I asked her as she approached, trying to be as polite as I could. There was definitely a non-zero chance that she'd been ordered to do just that.

"Not quite, though the matriarch has requested that three of your products be reserved for her. I'm assured you'll be compensated generously."

"And the meeting?" I asked.

"When you're done with this," she said, indicating the trading.

That was a relief, as was the fact that they didn't seem to want a fight. With how little the people here actually used their magic, I might have been able to fight one elder, but the five who'd arrived could most certainly have dealt with me, if for no other reason than the fact that they'd have more stamina. I did have a trick or two up my sleeve if it came to that, though.

She nodded to her companions, and all but one of them moved to speak to Isha. The younger elves, knowing that more serious parties had arrived, pulled back a bit. All of them knew that elders weren't to be crossed lightly. The leaders of Atal could easily have subdued even me had they wanted. Oma, having what she wanted, seemed content to let her fellows make their trades.

"It occurs to me that perhaps I should speak to you instead," said the man who'd held back as he looked at me. "Young Isha may be the one who trades for your group, but you're the one who made these heating crystals, no?"

My wife looked taken aback by that, and I was too. She'd been the one handling this up until now, the one who wanted to, the one I wanted to as well.

"No," I said in response.

"No?"

"No, I dislike negotiating trades intensely."

"And I'd much rather speak to those who are actually in charge of things, rather than some girl," he said flippantly.

I stood from the pool of water I'd been lounging in, letting it flow off me in rivulets as I released my hold on my magic. All around me the air filled with the power of the aura every spellcaster let off, pushed out by my anger until it flowed down from the tier I was on. Most of the time, I ignored auras, pushing them to the back of my mind as just another natural part of this world, like shadows or the smell of the wind, but when we were angry, we could loose them, and I did so now. The small green bubbles that were always around me now pushed out like a wave.

Those who lived here had likely never seen war, never had to fight against our own kind seriously, and never expected me to respond so harshly. After all, I'd been fairly laid back until now, but there were things I wouldn't stand for, and disrespecting Isha was on that list. The people around me saw that, and many began to pull back, eyes widening as I prepared to fight if I deemed it necessary.

"You should leave," I warned him.

"There will be no fighting here!" Oma shouted, moving between the two of us, flexing her own power as she put barriers into place. "Eren, you're out of line. Our guests told you who would handle the trades and were more than willing to engage with you properly."

"My apologies, Oma," he said, bowing slightly as he took a step back.

"And you," the diminutive woman said, turning to me. "You are a guest here, and should have let me handle that. This place is too important for you to be fighting here, regardless of the reasons."

"Understood," I said with a bow of my head. It rankled me, but she was the one in charge of this area, so she could enforce her rules, and I was a guest here.

Eren turned toward Isha, who was looking at him with a small scowl. "Would you be willing . . ."

"Why would you speak to me, Elder Eren? I'm just some girl," she said with envenomed sweetness.

"I suppose that settles that," Oma said, clearly indicating that the other elder should leave.

After he'd left, one of the others who'd come with Oma laughed under her breath. Apparently, Eren wasn't well liked by his contemporaries.

Isha continued with her trading, managing to get a good stock of the lights they used here and some other trinkets that were honestly of little value to me. Icehome, it seemed, had its own form of dyes that were more vivid than what could easily be made back in Atal, and a few unique herbs from mushrooms or the small plants that dotted the icy tundra that surrounded us. She secured ample amounts of those and even a recipe for a magical tattoo ink that served to bolster one's resistance to cold, not something I had in my repertoire but would surely be of value to someone.

Once she was all done, Oma took me to go see the leader of Icehome. Technically, Chien still had a few of his trinkets to trade, but we didn't actually know where he'd gone off to, and I didn't really expect to see him for a while anyway. He could handle it, but I hoped he didn't get involved with that other elder.

CHAPTER 23

THE MATRIARCH'S THRONE ROOM

Oma led me upward, higher and higher into Icehome. Most of the important people lived low, below the rock line, where it was warmer, where the stones insulated better, but not the leader. No, she lived above. I was surprised when we got to a ramp that led us further upward, somewhere I'd not yet been, a ramp that corkscrewed through the glacier.

I knew we'd arrived when a pair of thick, blue-white doors opened up before me. They were significantly smoother than the rest of the doors I'd seen in Icehome, but this was an ancient after all. They stood out, pale against the surrounding deeper blues of the glacial ice, and it seemed intentional.

As the twin doors swung open, seemingly on their own but decidedly through someone pushing them with magic, I saw Matriarch Neera sitting regally on a throne of ice. She'd covered her seat with furs at least, and there were more on the floor before her, but here and there the frozen water peeked out.

The room wasn't cold, as one might have expected inside a glacier. As a point of fact, it was warm, pleasant heat radiating from several of the people present—the advisors and direct subordinates of the oldest elf present.

Matriarch Neera looked almost cute, smaller than most adult elves and with her hair done up in complex braids and crystals of blue and white entwined within. Her dress was flowy, made of several layers, almost like some kind of fabric, but from here I could tell that it wasn't something so plain as that. Rather it looked to be some form of fur, only so fine and so thin that it moved like nothing I'd ever seen. It gave her the look of one of the fictional magical girls from Earth. I briefly wondered if she was cold, since the dress was quite a bit shorter than what one would normally wear in this environment.

"So, you are the young man causing such a ruckus in my home," she said lightly as I approached.

"Ah, forgive me Matriarch. I have been told that I lack subtlety." The millennia-old girl giggled at that, a high, tinkling sound incongruous with the destructive potential of any of our kind who reached her age.

"I believe I requested certain goods from you as well?" she said, holding out a hand.

I took out the three stones she'd ordered. Sure, she could take them and give me nothing. I wouldn't really be out much, after all. If I wanted more, I would just make them. Rather than have me approach her throne, the crystals—suspended in their diamond cases—floated forward, circling around playfully before her. I could feel the mana wafting off of her, blue eyes locked on her new toys.

"This is interesting work," she commented after a few moments.

"Thank you," I said. "Your subjects seem quite keen to have their own heat sources."

"No, not that," she said. "The little stones you've suspended them in. We could easily have more heating stones if we wanted, but these little clear gems—I've never seen their like before."

"If you could get them, then why don't you?" I asked, confused. I knew it was a great thing for her people to do, a huge achievement.

"You don't know about us, child," she replied. "That much is clear. Very well, I'll take some time to teach you. Well, before my time we lived in the mountains all over this continent, but in doing so we were divided, separated, weak. By the time my predecessor took over our tribe, there were almost none of us left, but he gathered what he could and tried to take territory, good land that would support us."

"And he brought you here?"

"No, he lost nearly all of his warriors, almost everything. The remnants settled here, chased to the ends of the world by our enemies. At that time I was the only elder, the last, and if I'm being honest, I was also the weakest of them. Still, I managed to build this place, to expand it, and once I'd become strong enough, I got the heating stone you saw down below."

"You never tried to leave?"

"We're too weak. We have too few strong fighters to take the territory from any of the other ancients, and while some of my people might be able to leave, they would be highly intolerant of another ancient ruling them. Perhaps if we'd been allies or lovers before attaining our age, but not now."

"If you want stronger fighters, you can start with the heating room. It's keeping them pathetically weak." That was one of the things that bothered me most; it was almost criminal in my eyes.

She sighed, almost tired. "Teaching them and sending them out would make them stronger, but I have so few. I need numbers before anything can happen, numbers I simply don't have. Perhaps you hate it, think me cruel for not encouraging their growth, but that growth is dangerous. Surely you know this? I want my people to thrive, and for that, we'll need more than we have now. It's why I meet with everyone who goes to get a heating stone, to tell them not to get more, and inform them of the consequences if they do. Most of them understand in the end, but I doubt you care."

I backed down. After all, it wasn't really my business, was it? And she did seem to have her people's best interests in mind, rather than some evil plot.

"I suppose. I am just here to give you a message."

"Very well, what is it?"

"Atal and Cino are dead."

For the first time since I got here she actually seemed bothered. "Both of them?! How?"

"Cino killed Atal, then died himself." I didn't feel like elaborating, didn't want her to feel threatened.

"I . . . see, and their lands?" A valid question if she'd been stuck up here with her people.

"No ancient has claimed them. I know that in Atal's city there is much stress about that."

"Yes, I would assume so . . . I really shouldn't have delayed you."

"Are you going to try and take them?"

"Perhaps I'll take Cino's lands. Protected as they are it would be good, and surrounded by mountains, but there will be much to do first, so much."

"Very well, that was all I needed to say, so if there's nothing else . . ."

"There is. Did you not hear me ask about this stone? Where did it come from? How did you make it?"

"The heating stone?"

"No child, the clear one. I want to know about it."

"That is a very private matter, one I would rather not share."

She frowned, almost a pout. "I would give you much for it, very much."

"That secret is not for sale, I'm afraid."

"I could force you, you know?"

"You could," I said. "I know you could, and you'd probably succeed, but I would be your enemy afterward." As I spoke, I prepared to act. The trick I'd readied for this very situation, one she'd fallen into.

"Should I fear you?"

"You never asked who killed Cino."

She froze at my words, froze and sat back, looking at me intently. I knew that ancients didn't get to their age through foolish actions, and while she might be able to smite me where I stood, she might not. After a second of thinking she breathed out.

"Perhaps you did, perhaps you could again, perhaps not, but you might be a useful ally too, no? You could stay, if your words are true, and with your abilities, I would treat you well."

"And if I say no?"

"Then you may leave as you came, in peace."

"I would like to leave in peace."

"Very well." She snapped her fingers, and one of her aides approached. "See to it our guest is paid for his goods and allowed to leave when he is ready."

I didn't relax until I was several floors down, well away from the matriarch. It was a relief I'd not had to fight her, because while she'd taken those crystals from me, and I was sure I could have detonated them from where I stood nearby, I wasn't sure it would have beaten her. A trick pulled successfully once was one thing, but that was still the only way I had to reliably beat someone so much stronger than me, and I didn't want to use it too many times.

CHAPTER 24

ANGRY ISHA

Matriarch Neera was generous, providing enough wood for us to make a proper sled and loading it down with a mixture of trading goods and slightly magical compounds. These included several antlers, pelts that seemed to never get even slightly wet, and a blend of herbs used in tattooing inks and the like.

I'd never had much to do with magical materials, or rather those that were already doing things, other than my brief lessons in tattooing, but they still held tons of value. Even if I'd never seen many of them, I knew that there were many types of magical beasts and plants that came about rarely and had fantastical powers. Sadly, most of what I'd seen, except the weird shadowy beasts that had once attacked my home village, had very minor effects overall and seemed very similar to some of the weird biology of Earth.

Isha added her items to the sled, but Chien had been cagey. I didn't know what his trades had been, but I had some ideas based on what I knew about him. As we approached the door leaving Icehome, a girl appeared near the back of the entry chamber, looking around.

"Shit, we gotta go, boss," he said, hurrying out the exit.

"What did you do?" I asked as I began pulling the sled.

"Don't worry, it'll be fine," he replied. "We just need to go."

"Chien . . ."

As we began to move through the snow, flakes falling around us, he whispered, "Look, I may have made some mistakes, and she might think that I'm significantly more interested in staying here than I am, and . . ."

"And you didn't have the guts to tell her the truth?" Isha accused, looking disgusted.

"She was trying to get me to meet her family!" he said, trying to be quiet while shouting at the same time. We still weren't far enough from the hive's doorway and close enough that others coming in and out could hear us. "What was I supposed to do when she went to get her parents, huh?"

"Stop her, and explain things properly, obviously!" Isha reached for his ear, but my assistant ducked her hand, pulling ahead. "Come back here right this moment! You're going back and fixing this right now!"

"No, I am not," Chien retorted. "She'll be fine, it'll all be fine, you'll see. Sure, she'll mope for a bit, but that girl wasn't dense. I'm sure she'll understand . . . eventually." Isha tried to chase him, but Chien simply had longer legs, and unless they began to sling spells at one another, there really wasn't much to worry about.

I kept my mouth shut. Sure, what Chien was doing was wrong, but I'd be a liar if I said I didn't understand. He didn't want to get involved, to get tied down. The girl in question hadn't meant anything to him, even if she'd thought she had, and he was running rather than explaining that to her and possibly her angry relatives.

I was also sure it would come back to bite him in the ass one day. These things tended to; we lived long lives.

The two of them were so busy bickering that they hardly noticed as we pulled away from Icehome, getting further and further from the large settlement. Our working plan was to travel south and then east, since I was told there was a coast that way, and hopefully a way out of this awful tundra. How far would it be? I didn't rightly know, but it could take weeks and weeks, even if we went quickly. We weren't in any rush, though. Things would take as long as they took.

That first night away from Icehome, the change in our preparations showed itself in how great it was. The little igloo we made from the snow and ice wasn't cold, but pleasantly warm, one of the heating stones we'd reserved filling it with hot air. With the furs we'd gained, our beds were several times better than they'd been, and food was both plentiful and tasty compared to what it had been. The fact that Isha was still angry with Chien put a damper on things, though. Shooting him glares the whole night and even adding me to her list when she realized that I wasn't going to do anything about it.

"You can't think he's right," she complained as she joined me in our bed.

"I don't."

"But you're not going to say anything to him?"

"He's an adult," I said. "He can make mistakes if he wants to. I'm certainly no paragon of morals to tell him what he must do."

"How can you say that with all the people you've saved?" she asked, taking my face in her hands and making me look her in the eyes.

"All the people I've killed," I responded.

"Sometimes we have to kill, but I know you, Elian. I know you hate hurting people. I know you didn't want to do those things, but you had to, because of what would have happened if you hadn't. Can you seriously tell me that you enjoyed hurting people?"

"I don't, but it's not the same."

"Sometimes good people have to do things they hate to stop evil. You could have caused lots more trouble back there in Icehome, and we both know it. You could have done so much more, but what did you do? You helped people; you gave them means to keep themselves safe while teaching them what you could. Sure, it irritated the people in charge, but you didn't try to lead some sort of rampage, or just up and tell them they were being wronged. Instead you took a gentler path."

"You see more good in me than I do, love." My thoughts went back to the children Cino had used, and how I'd failed to save them, failed to help them, how I'd failed so many times and all the pain that came from those failures.

"Someone has to, but remember this—if you were a monster, you wouldn't really care about harming others, would you?"

In response I just kissed her on her forehead, for that was better than any words I had.

"Which is why you should tell Chien off," she complained.

"I think we're a bit beyond going back to apologize," I retorted.

"Maybe, but he should know not to bloody do it again. He probably does, but he'll listen better if it's you who points it out."

"Let's not talk about this anymore tonight," I said, kissing her lightly.

"Fine." With that word she turned her back to me, looking out the other side of the bed angrily. It seemed I wouldn't be getting any peace tonight.

CHAPTER 25

THE GAP

After a few days, I pulled Chien to the side.

"You know I care for you, right Chien?"

"Yeah, boss, what's up."

"Please don't ever do a repeat of your actions in Icehome again. I'd rather have peace with Isha."

"Yeah, me too. Did you notice how she's making only the foods she knows I hate?" he asked. Isha, with her ability to conjure certain foods into existence, generally took care of most of the cooking.

"Yeah, yeah I did." It wasn't lost on me that those were also some of my least favorite foods.

"So, we're letting her win?"

"It's not about winning or losing. She's right to be unhappy with you. You never win against someone you care about, because then they have to lose, you merely fix things, so please try to fix things, because I care about both of you, and this is foolishness."

We traveled in near silence day after day, the pale ice and bleak landscape not much to inspire conversation. Added to that that my two companions were fighting, and it made things boring indeed. Rocks and gulleys passed, small points of black in the white background, sometimes with pale blue or light green sprigs of growth dotting them.

Over our travels I manage to do some hunting, taking out small hares periodically. Those at least added a bit of fresh meat to our diet, beating the smoked rations we had. Unfortunately, there weren't really any nuts or trees to speak of, nor the roots I had grown fond of over the course of my life. Even fish and seafood, something I'd not always loved but had come to appreciate while living in seaside Atal, was missing.

As we walked, I mused because I didn't know how people did it, living in a place like this. It was just so pale, and always the same. No seasons, no migrations. I had a hard time imagining myself living here long term. Maybe that was why the elves of Icehome had been so loath to do more than live in their hive. At least there they could entertain each other with games and stories; it's better than wandering the wastes. It was also clear that Neera had chosen the best part of the wastes for her home, because they were getting somehow bleaker.

We came upon a crevice in the ice—a shattered and jagged line crossing the landscape—about a week after I'd spoken with Chien.

"Looks deep," he said, chucking a small orb of light into the black canyon.

Chien's light sent a sparkling cascade bouncing between the walls, glittering like diamonds as it descended lower and lower.

"Decidedly deep," I agreed. "And I don't see an easy way around."

"Over?" he asked. The crack was about fifty feet across.

"Might be able to manage that spell, but I'm hesitant to try something new over something like this."

"What do you think then?" Isha asked, looking between us.

"I'll go north," I said pointing. "See if there's a way around, if not, we go south, it'll take us off course, but better that than trying something dangerous."

"Should we all go?" Chien asked.

"Nah, no point dragging everything along; it would just be needless work. I'll be back in a bit."

I hurried along the edge, looking down as I did. Could there be a monster here? I didn't know, but they did seem to like odd places, and this certainly was one, so it was possible. It was also possible that this thing was unstable, not somewhere I wanted to spend too much time, but there was no choice.

Twenty minutes was enough for me to see quite a bit of this thing, and no end in sight. Just as I was preparing to turn around, though, I saw some movement on the other side of the crevice. I squinted into the snowy landscape, and there it was, right on the precipice.

The creature in question was a bird, white on top with dark blue feathers underneath. If it had been black I would have called it a crow with the beak and rough size. The little bird, the only bird I'd seen on this plateau, looked at me curiously, blending in almost perfectly with the icy background.

"Caw!"

"No worries there, friend. I'm not here to hurt you," I said calmly to it, nodding.

After cawing at me a few more times and seeming to realize that I didn't care to mess with it, the little avian turned back to the cliffside and began to peck, eventually dislodging, and promptly eating, a shard of ice.

"Magic animals are weird," I declared to the universe at large. At least it didn't seem aggressive.

I turned to make my way back to my companions. Sure, I could keep going out of the way, but eventually we'd find the end of this gash in the ice, and it wasn't like we were in a huge rush. As I got nearer, I slowed, seeing them sitting there, apparently deep in conversation. I slowed my run down to a slow stroll. They'd been arguing, and if they were now chatting, that could only be good, probably.

Even though I all but stopped, I was eventually noticed by my companions, who waved me over. They were sitting back-to-back on the sled, and as I came near they looked at me expectantly.

"Anything good?" Isha asked.

"Sadly no. Looks like we'll just have to go around."

Chien just shrugged like it made no difference to him and we continued. Their attitude had changed, though, and where there'd been silence, they now started up a game, looking for familiar scenes in the sparkling ice or the waves of the snow. Was everything always going to be all right between them? Well, probably not. Everyone argued sometimes, but they were trying, and trying was the important thing.

Throughout the day we saw a few more of the strange little birds. The closest ones to us flew off, hopping away or flying to the other side of the crevice or down into it. It was weird, but since they weren't hurting anything, we were happy enough to leave them alone. These things had to be at least somewhat magical, so I didn't want to risk that they were as smart as actual crows and might hold a grudge.

That night our little shelter was brighter than it had been since leaving Icehome. Rather than quietly sleeping, we chatted well into the evening. Isha and Chien didn't tell me what had transpired between them, but it didn't much matter. As we finally put away our lights and went to bed, there was a tapping on the roof of our ice hut. First it started in one place, then another, and another. Soon it sounded like all around us little hammers were slamming into our shelter.

CHAPTER 26

BATTLE OF THE BIRDS

Pecking, scratching, and tapping. The noises filtered down to us through the shelter like a hard rain. This, however, was a rain of beaks, of potentially very intelligent animals. I really just wanted the birds to go away, but the chances of that at this juncture seemed low.

"They're ripping up the shelter!" Chien yelled.

"But why?!" Isha asked.

"They eat ice, particularly the edges of the ice," I said. "Maybe they find it easier to take on things that have edges already, and if that's the case, our little hut is perfect for them. They're probably hungry, and I'd wager they had a good hand in making that crevice."

"What do we do, boss?"

"Pack everything quickly, and get ready."

I threw up a bubble around us as I dressed. It was cold out there, and I didn't want to get a face full of icy wind or have this hut collapse on us. It was fortunate that I did too, as they quickly made a hole, a pair of eyes peeking through and looking down.

"CAW!" said the surprised looking bird, peering in at us. The noise increased, sounding like we were caught in a hailstorm of beaks. There was cracking as, bit by bit, our shelter collapsed under the weight of the pecking, and I could see them—hundreds, maybe even thousands of the little beasts—munching away at our shelter.

The ice sloughed away, disappearing into the gullets of the ice. There were now crows and piles of ice around what used to be our shelter.

Chien looked at me. "Fight?"

"I don't think they're after us, just the ice," I replied right before one of them began pecking at my shield bubble. "Then again, I could be wrong. Let me try to be nice first."

Who knew if the bird-brains thought my shield was just some really hard, delicious ice, or if they actually wanted to fight, but I wasn't willing to find out. I started with a pulse, trying to push them back without being violent.

That was apparently a mistake as the enraged flock cawed loudly before one of them made a strange movement, sending several of its feathers at us like icy darts. One led to several, led to dozens, led to all of them.

"All right, no more nice guy. Hit 'em hard!"

Chien and I both let loose a barrage of darts—fire from me, and force from him—all of them striking into the horde. Of course, Isha outdid both of us, screaming loudly at them and taking whole sections down. Apparently, they didn't have much defense against sound, as wings and beaks simply shattered under the auditory assault.

As I watched one of the birds I'd struck with fire struggle on the ground, I noticed bits and pieces of the others were attracted to it like iron shavings to a magnet. Seconds passed, and it began to form into some unholy, frozen abomination.

"Don't use fire!" I shouted.

"You were the only one doing that!" Chien replied.

Several of the beasts I thought I'd taken down rose, excess wings, beaks, feathers, and strangely shaped appendages sticking out at odd angles. Of course they could still fly. It was only natural, right? As they rose into the air, we bombarded the now larger creatures, sending them flapping with waves of sound and physical force.

"Abso-fucking-lutely not!" I screamed. I blasted another with the hardest kinetic bolt I could manage as it tried to rise from the ground. We were not having any more eldritch ice bird abominations here today. That was a hard no.

The battle felt like it had gone on for hours, though realistically, it'd probably only been a few minutes when the last living birds decided to retreat, ceding the field to us. Everywhere I looked there were bits of them, feathers and broken bodies littering the ground. A few were still moving, making pained noises as their injuries prevented them from rising. We quickly went about putting them out of their misery. Dangerous or not, they were living things and shouldn't be made to suffer needlessly.

"All right," I said to my sweat-soaked companions, "I vote we get as far away from here as possible before remaking camp."

"I'll second that," Isha chimed in.

"Thirded."

"Good, it's unanimous then. I'd rather lose the sleep than have that happen ever again."

Even as I spoke I noted the place mentally. Sure, I didn't want to risk carrying these monsters away with us now, but in the future, who knew? They seemed fairly tame . . . at first at least, and it might be possible to use them one day. Not today, though, as there was no chance I was going to try and capture and carry those things off now that they'd been all worked up, even if I had a way, which I didn't.

We fled to the south, hoping to find our way across, agreeing that if we couldn't, we'd go back west to get away from here before continuing. As a hope of speeding things along, we all hopped on the sled and I propelled it with magic. The sensation was odd. Trying to move something you were on was subtly disorienting, but it was possible. Something I'd have to note of if I ever wanted to fly properly, which I did one day.

A small murder of the ice crows followed us at a distance, watching our moves and shadowing from high above. None got too close, though. It seemed they realized we were dangerous and wanted nothing more to do with us. Those that were munching away at the crevice itself quickly dispersed into the air as we approached, warned off by a series of caws from our escorts. That boded poorly for how smart these things actually were if they were doing something that complex. At least they weren't using tools, yet.

All night and day we traveled, Chien occasionally switching out with me so I could regain mana. We even had to get out and push a few times, but after far too long we found the far end of the canyon and managed to make our way across it. How long had these things been here? How did the ice keep coming back? How many were there? I didn't know and didn't need to know. All I wanted was to get past this blockade and back to our mission, long though it may be.

Once we actually started moving away, the birds only followed us for a bit longer. They could see we were leaving their territory behind, having not attacked any more since our battle, and seemed content once it was clear we wouldn't be hunting them down today.

We even managed to find outcroppings with a good overhang before going to sleep, only having to use snow (decidedly not ice) to form a doorway. All of us were exhausted, and as I slept, I had nightmares, dreams of hundred-foot-tall balls of flapping wings and ice bearing down on us with avian hatred. Those alone were enough to make me wake several times in a cold sweat, something my companions seemed to do a few times themselves.

CHAPTER 27

OFF THE ICE

After weeks of travel we discovered a few things. One, that riding on the sled was far, far, faster than any other method of travel, and two, I really needed to work on doing more magic. There was never enough, and the only way to get better at it was to do more. Using the sled was tiring, exhausting even, but with the speed we were traveling, it was so worth it that none of us wanted to stop.

Even Chien got in on the sledding action, but we found that he was much weaker than I, something I'd expected, but never had full confirmation. I wondered if it had something to do with my other-worldly origin, or if I just practiced more. Even though, admittedly, I still needed more practice.

Weeks passed, and as with anything, we improved. The spells were worked out, and the tricks of the trade to smooth things out were cleaned up. We hit the snowy ground over a dozen times, only for Isha to fix us up. As we moved, we ate through our supplies, literally and figuratively, and if not for Isha's ability to magic food into existence, we might have been struggling.

"Good shot," I told Chien as he sniped a hare with a small kinetic bolt.

"Thanks, keep an eye out while I clean it?"

"Sure." We were now keeping watch whenever we stopped for even a moment, though we'd not had any experiences with more magical fauna.

His cuts were exact, quick and practiced. We all knew how to do it now, but that didn't mean we were all good at it. Ironically, I was probably the worst of us when it came to cleaning animals and all other manner of outdoors skills. I just did it via magic, skipping all the hard parts.

"How far you think we are?"

"Dunno, Chien, probably something we should have asked before heading out, but I can't imagine it's much further. Still think it's a minor miracle we found the others when we did. We could have wandered out on the ice for years if we'd not stumbled upon them."

"I'm not staying out here for years," Isha chimed in.

"I doubt we'll take that long." I didn't say it, but we must have traveled over a thousand miles, so there was no way it could be that much further until we made it to the far side of the continent, I hoped.

Hopeful thoughts aside, there really was only one way to get through this, and that was simply to get through this. That said, I was seeing some more rocks and scrub, which could only be a good sign as far as I was concerned.

The next morning the horizon looked odd to me, and as we got closer and closer, it became apparent that there was a large change. The edge of the world, which had been flat with only the smallest of bumps, began to rise on one side while falling away on the other.

"Is that what I think it is?" Chien shouted.

"Don't jinx it," Isha and I yelled at him.

It was, though, and as we moved closer we found the edge of the plateau. The world below us spread out, clouds parting until below us a strip of green was revealed. To one side rose a line of high mountains, and to the other the pristine blue of the ocean. Between the two lay a line, perhaps only a few miles wide, of verdant land, small trees, and lush grasses, with the occasional ribbon of silver sliding down the mountains to water the coast.

"Well, how do we get down?" Isha asked, looking around for an answer.

We'd managed to find a perfect spot on our way in, hidden behind a waterfall, but there were no such features nearby, nor were there any spots that stood out from the sheer drop. We went up and down the plateau for a bit, but with the small area that we actually wanted to be in, there was a very finite number of places to look. Could we have found something eventually? Probably.

"I have an idea," I finally said.

"Okay," my companions agreed.

"Get in the sled."

They obliged, and I hopped on the back before catapulting us over the edge.

Chien let off a very imaginative series of oaths, curses, and obscenities. Isha mostly screamed. Mostly that was just distracting as I wrapped my magic around us and tried to pull upward. The sensation was still odd and uncomfortable, but with the practice, it worked, slowing us significantly.

The landing was . . . a landing. The runners from the sled shattered when we hit, but with the layers of stuff packed in, they were the only casualties, and it wasn't like they were that thick anyway. I went flying, jarred by the impact and sent on a mad tumble from the sled. Chien and Isha managed to stay with our things.

"Elian, what were you thinking?!" Isha screamed, grabbing a fur from the pile and advancing upon me. It was easy to tell when she was really angry because she started using my childhood name again.

"That we'd probably be fine," I replied to my displeased significant other.

"Probably?!"

I covered my ears. People in this world always went for the ears when they were angry. Isha didn't disappoint, slapping me with the little rabbit fur vigorously, mostly upon the head. She eventually ran out of steam, huffing and puffing as she tired herself out.

"Were you not going to help?" I asked Chien as she stalked away; his response was to throw a stick at me, which was fair, I supposed.

As soon as I was back up and moving, we had things to sort through. The sled was mostly a bust, which was fine, as there were now a few trees in easy enough reach. None were huge, but they'd serve to make little woodworking projects. We were also well versed in creating such things, so it wasn't too much of a chore to rebuild.

Interestingly, much of the wood here was some form of either ironwood or birch. I tried to remember if the leaves matched what I'd known from my previous life, but honestly I'd never really known what they were supposed to look like, mostly paying attention to the bark. They looked to match as far as I could tell, but my knowledge, while perfect for what I could remember, didn't tell me about things I'd never looked at.

I considered making wheels, but wheels did best with roads, and roads we did not have. I wasn't even sure if anyone lived on this side of the mountains. That could be something to bring into Atal when I finally returned. Wheels and balloons, maybe. I liked balloons. Making them didn't need nearly as much complex math as a plane, and I was pretty sure that with magic we could make them far better than anyone had on Earth.

Soon enough, I had the sled rebuilt, the stuff repacked, and my significant other mollified enough that we could begin moving south once more. We all shed our coats and other layers, going back to the leafy clothing provided to us before we'd gone to find Neera. The temperature was at least nice now, the quick drop having rapidly brought us out of the ice and into a far more reasonable climate.

"Let's go," Isha said, leaving me to pull the sled.

CHAPTER 28

COASTAL FOREST

There was a certain light joy to this little coastline. It was odd to me that it was so small, barely going up to the mountains before steeply climbing, but I knew neither enough about geography nor about how magic might interact with it to know if it was normal. It was pleasant, though, for you could always smell the subtle salt on the wind and find nearby shade. Odder still was that the floor of the forest wasn't all sand, though that was more welcome than I could easily state; I hated sand.

Isha pouted, Chien walked silently, and I pulled our little sled, either with magic or muscles. I had the feeling that both were still rather irked at me for my stunt at the cliff, but what could you do? It would've taken days and days for us to try and climb down slowly, and I simply wasn't willing to wait that long; nor did we have the right equipment.

"Well, at least it's not cold," I said after a while.

"True," Chien said. "Does it have something to do with us being closer to the sea, or not as high up?"

"Yes, the air gets cooler as you go higher up, at least most of the time. There are a lot of factors."

He accepted it with a shrug. "Okay, boss, if you say so."

"You shouldn't just take my word for it," I said, lugging up the rope to conserve mana. "You should test it. I mean, I think I'm right, but who knows about everything? I could be wrong at times, or just not know. It will happen as time goes on."

"How would I test that?"

"You know, that's a good question. Think on it for a while and see if you can come up with something, then we can both test it. I mean, I think a lot of things, but I could be wrong about any or all of them."

He nodded once more and began to let his thoughts take him. That was good. I mean, there was every possibility I would die before we got far with this society, and if I did . . . well, it would be best if I could leave something behind for others, and the scientific method was one of the best things I could leave them. Even if I'd not taught something, that might manage to help them learn it.

All around us there were plants I'd never seen, flowers and trees slightly different from those back in Atal's area. Most interesting were some of the fruits, which hung heavy from trees. Some of them were as large or larger than coconuts, big balls hanging in the air. I wondered if they were edible, or if they'd need some treatment to become such. On the shore there were, of course, a few actual coconuts, or the local equivalent.

That first night we camped just inside the jungle, just off of the sand. Even in this world, sand flies were a menace, and none of us were willing to brave them while dreaming. Though, as the sun set to the west, we watched it sink over the horizon, a novel experience.

For us, it was normally as the sun rose that it passed over the ocean, but on the opposite coast we could see the deep reds and purples rather than the pinks and yellows of dawn.

As we prepared to return to the small shelter we'd made, I saw a light in the ocean, just a flicker, and only for a second. Then there was another, and another, and soon the ocean looked like a churning sea of stars. Each wave brought in more light, pale glows hanging in the waves, before taking it back out again.

"What is it?" Isha asked breathily, getting closer to see.

"I don't know," I responded, pulling nearer the waves.

"Is it safe?" Chien asked, and that brought both of us back to our senses and from the place where the water crashed into the sand.

"Good call," I said. "We don't' know if it's dangerous or not. Best to stay out of the water for now . . ."

For a while we watched the pretty colors, keeping well back upon the shore, until one of the lights stayed behind. Several more followed suit, each first sticking to the sand before moving upward along it.

Interested, I reached out with my magic, gently picking up one of the little glowing bits, before bringing it closer to look at it. We all gathered around to take a look. Upon the bit of sand I'd grabbed was a tiny crab, smaller than the nail of my pinky, and it was moving about. The animal didn't seem overly pleased to have been plucked from its place and was waving a minuscule claw around threateningly.

"It's so cute!" Isha said, her voice hitting octaves I'd seldom heard. "Look at you, you angry little man."

She tried to poke at it, and the crab pinched her finger, causing her to pull it back quickly from the unhappy crustacean with a yelp. Both Chien and I got a good laugh out of that, but it left a glowing mark upon her skin. Something that made me stop as soon as I saw it.

"Purge whatever that is," I said, flicking the crab back toward the sea, "and don't touch anything. It's probably poison of some kind."

Isha's eyes rose, and she began to sing, but the glowing spot didn't go away. It merely spread, from a pinprick to something the size of a letter on a page. Without hesitating I grabbed her hand, focusing my mana to quickly slice around it. She screamed loudly, but I held her in place. A toxin that spread when exposed to magic was no joke, and we didn't know what it would do.

"I'm sorry, love," I said. "Heal it again, and we need to get back from this shore." I could already see where the flowing bit of her flesh had fallen, and how there were lights now advancing toward it from the waves. The crabs seemed to know where the poison was and were seeking it out. I could only pray I'd gotten all of the effected region off quickly enough.

She sang as we retreated to the forest, and Chien looked at our shelter with a frown.

"Further in, boss?" he asked.

"All the way to the mountain," I said. "No risks."

We kept an eye on Isha, but it seemed we'd gotten lucky. There was a chunk of her pointer finger missing, and she was quite alarmed by her healing having initially failed, but she was safe. With the sled in tow, we retreated up to the base of the mountain, and I made a note to keep well away from the shore, at least at night.

Over the next few days we walked, trying to find anything that would supplement our rapidly dwindling supplies, but animals were sparse on the ground here. I even resorted to going nearer to the ocean, looking for any fish that might be swimming around. That was of limited use, as I wasn't willing to get in the water, and we weren't even sure what around here was edible.

About a week in, we found something. At a place where the shore pulled in to make a small cove, there were huts raised above the shore on poles that were sunk deep. Each had a small odd-looking thing at the base, but there were elves going about their business along the shore and around the houses. A few even looked up as we approached, waving us inward.

CHAPTER 29

SEASIDE VILLAGE

G ood that you removed the flesh when you did," the elder of the little seaside village said. He barely had a white hair upon his head, but was amenable enough. "It's not that dangerous, but it attracts the crabs and they'll swarm. They're persistent too."

We'd arrived here a few hours ago, and while we spoke, a child with spots all along her skin sat by us in the elder's home. The glowing bits didn't seem to hurt, but there were only two choices—to let the venom fade on its own, or to cut it away. Nobody wanted to cut a child, so the answer was clear, time and time alone.

"Thank you for sharing what you know," I said. "Is there any other beast we should know of in the area?"

"Few," he replied. "From the waters sometimes we get monstrous creatures, but they are mercifully few here. Further to the south near the flaming mountains, there are more, and I'd advise you to avoid them, unless you are keen to hunt the beasts as so many who come down from the plateau are."

"No, hunting isn't the goal of our expedition. Tell me, though, if Neera and her people know of you, which I assume they do, why do none come here to try and take the land?"

"Sure, we know them, and often their people who try to get their little heating stones come by, but there's nowhere near enough forest here for them all to live. The matriarch has her lands, which can support her population, but if they came here, most would starve."

That tracked. The village here was small, maybe ten huts, with less than fifty people total. I also suspected that they were heavily influenced by their more northern neighbors. My reasoning? They were paler, not as pale as those of Icehome, but close, and covered much of their skin when outside. If I had to guess, the two populations had a lot of overlap, either from those who passed through, or from this one being an outgrowth of the other.

"Fair."

Beside us, Isha was playing with the young girl, who seemed rather bored with being cooped up.

"You know I got one too, right here on my finger," she told the child.

"Yeah, I fell in the water at night," the little girl said. "Mommy told me to stay back, but they're pretty. You don't have spots, though?"

"No, had to cut away the light before it could spread; it hurt bad."

"I have to stay here 'til they go away. Mommy said she would cut them off if it were just one, but too many is bad. My auntie got one too when she pulled me out of the water, and they just cut hers away and healed it."

The kid seemed well enough, if bored. Perhaps I could fashion some checkers or chess pieces for her. It wasn't like it would be much of a challenge, and it would at least give her something to do. My understanding was that it would take around a week for the venom to fade completely, and until it did, every night the crabs would swarm around anything effected. Ostensibly, the reason the little girl was having to stay here was so the elder could keep the animals back, if any managed to get close.

I finished up my conversation, and we were invited to a feast that evening, some tradition for guests. I wouldn't say no to free food. It would also give us a great chance to see what people ate around here. The local fruits were unknown to us, and knowing those would be a huge boon. I'd told the elder of Atal's and Cino's deaths, but it wasn't like it really affected him at all. This little village was the definition of rural, far from any large settlements and the large-scale politics of the world. It reminded me of home in a lot of ways.

Then again, there were a lot of differences. I didn't know why they did it, but the people here had built over the sand, and even below the waterline, on poles sunk into the sand, with the homes built atop them. Walkways crisscrossed the few homes, with one leading to the ground. For whatever reason, elves liked to be up in trees or in weird places. Humans, I guessed, wouldn't have ever considered some of these odd housing arrangements.

While we waited for the evening meal, I moved into the woods, heading up toward the mountains. There was no reason not to help the little girl with some games, so I would. The walk to the stone sentinels that loomed high wasn't long, and there were plenty of rocks of various colors that I could use.

By the time I'd taken things in hand and made both a board and some pieces, it was time to return to the village. The sun was setting, and I didn't want to be caught out if things went wrong. As I did so, I briefly wondered where my assistant had run off to.

It turned out I was just in time for the festivities and was greeted by the sound of happy chatter and the smell of food. All of it was happening around the elder's house, being that his hut was the largest of them all—the typical privilege of the strong. He waved as I came near, gesturing for me to sit around a small improvised table made of leaves.

"Welcome back, my friend," he said. "Please, eat, join us."

The large fruit we'd seen appeared to be something akin to breadfruit, and after being cooked were cut open and served in their shells. This was one of the main foods, with everything else being added to it, like putting fish or sauces onto rolls. The texture was weird, but it tasted subtly sweet and was quite filling.

I'd worried about Chien getting into some nonsense, but no, he was sitting between two other men and was deep in discussion about woodworking. They seemed keen, and being that the people here were using slightly more advanced techniques than we had originally had in Atal, this indicated that they would likely catch on quickly. Isha stayed with the child, and I slipped the board over to her. She'd know what to do, and she smiled at me. Looks like I might just be forgiven for throwing us off of that cliff.

Below us the phosphorescent crabs swarmed, attracted to the injured girl. Something about the pylons repelled them, though, some kind of layer on them that the creatures couldn't stand.

"Don't worry, they won't come up here," the elder said as I looked down.

"What's repelling them?"

"A mixture of things, mostly a goo from certain fish, suspended in tree sap. Has to stay wet to work, but it has served well for a long time. You can rest tonight."

I liked these people. They were decent.

CHAPTER 30

VOLCANIC

As the night wore on and people went to bed I found myself sitting beside the village elder, looking out over the softly crashing waves at the moon.

"I want to ask you for a favor," he said, looking at me.

"What's that?"

"Not agreeing first," he said. "Someone's asked for a favor before then, I take it?"

"We've had a long journey."

"Haha, well, for this one I don't need you to come back, and it's on your way."

"You still haven't told me what the favor is."

"Very well," the elder said, sighing. "As you travel south, the mountains change; some of them spit fire. Within these ranges are a number of fairly dangerous beasts, but there's one mountain in particular—don't worry you won't miss it—that I'd like you to look into. We always try to keep an eye on it, but nobody's been by in a while."

"You said I didn't need to come back. How exactly are you supposed to learn what we find if we don't?" I was beginning to see some problems with his request. I wasn't writing it off, but I really didn't want to backtrack when we were close to finishing this awful mission.

"Simple," he replied. "There is another village just before you hit the swamps. Tell them. I'm sure they'll be thankful, and if there's any immediate danger, they may well do something about it. If there's not, then the report can make it to me whenever it does."

"And what exactly do you need me to do?"

"Get as close as you can, see what you can. I'm not expecting much, but that place spawns beasts like the ocean makes fish. Just having someone put eyes on the mountain itself will be enough."

"Very well," I said. "I can't promise that I'll get close, but I'll look, see what I can."

"Thank you."

The next morning we set off, our hosts having given us more than we could imagine. It wasn't just the supplies we traded for, though that was some of it, but the knowledge. We now knew about several plants that could be easily harvested for food. The breadfruit was my personal favorite, and I wondered if they could be transplanted back to Atal. As an attempt, I filled one of my pockets with seeds so we could try.

Our trip was almost relaxing. We stayed mostly toward the mountain side of the little strip of land, wanting to avoid anything nasty coming from the ocean, but sometimes we'd take a day to walk along the shore instead. With the strip of good land only a few miles wide, it wasn't much of a challenge to change if we wanted.

Once or twice more we found small villages, and they were much like the first. Each was widely spread out from the others, making sure that there was no competition between them, but all were friendly. The people here lived simple lives, with few enemies and only the occasional attack from monsters, while their own slow birthrate kept them from covering the land.

We also started to see some changes in the ground. The forests seemed denser and more fertile, and the sands changed from a pale white to nearly black over the course of a couple of weeks. The plants, at least, were much the same, but they grew larger, taller, thicker. Knowing there were volcanoes somewhere nearby, it was likely the effect of the soil being brought up from that, but we'd yet to see one of them at that point. The lands were also getting wider, slowly expanding from a couple of miles to around ten, and then further. The mountains were still close, ever looming over us, but it seemed as if each day they fled further from the shore.

I almost didn't notice the first of them when they came into view, only realizing it when Chien pointed it out.

"Hey boss, is that what they were talking about?" he said, nodding toward one of the mountains.

"Maybe."

The sentinel was barren, covered in black rocks and shorter than those around it. As the sun set that night, we saw more too. Rather than rivers of water that I'd come to expect, this one had a few small reddish lines of magma slowly spilling down from it. At the base were clouds, ostensibly where those flows met water, but I couldn't see them from our vantage point.

"Why is it glowing?" Isha asked.

"Because there's melted rock flowing down the side of it."

That put both of my companions on the back foot. They obviously knew that things could be melted like that because I was a smith by trade. They also understood just how difficult it was to achieve these temperatures, with massive amounts of time and effort going into melting even small amounts of metal.

"Can we forge anything from it or in it?" Chien asked, still thinking business.

"Doubtful, though there may be some interesting rocks nearby from where it cools. We should look for those."

That night I began working on floating above ground. Flying like a bird was probably still out of the question for me, but I could at least try the basics of going up and forward, something we might need. Nobody had said anything, but what if one of those lava flows ended up making it all the way to the shore? I didn't have a boat. As a point of fact, I'd never seen a proper seafaring vessel at all, only small rafts and canoes.

The next day as we traveled, we got nearer to the volcano, trying to get a better look at it, and as we did, we began to see things. First were sections of new land, places where the old flows had hardened into fresh rock, smooth and devoid of life. Then, as we neared one of the rivers of lava, I spotted movement. It was subtle and far off, but I stopped our group.

"What is it?" Isha asked.

"I don't know," I said. "Something by the river there."

"I can't see anything," Chien said.

"Just saw it for a second. We really need a better way to see them . . ." I lamented, knowing that binoculars would be wonderful right about now.

"What about that bending light thing?" Chien asked.

I'd tried to give the kid as good an education as I thought he could understand, and years ago he'd asked about water. Why did water do weird things to the angle when you saw stuff? Everyone knew, because they could all see in calm rivers and streams, the way the light rippled. I'd not gone too deep into it, simply telling him that light could bend, but he remembered. Frankly, I was stunned that he'd thought of it.

"What? You said it messed with how you saw things, right?"

"Yeah . . . might be best if we tried it like this," I said, drawing a simple diagram for him. "Want to give it a go? It's your idea after all."

With a nod he did just that, warping the area before him into a lens. I sat back, looking on in pride as my apprentice did something I'd not suggested. Was this what having a child was like? No, this wasn't quite that deep, but there was a smile on my face as I watched him grow, giving us something to look through. It was blurry, and decidedly angled along the edges, but he made a wonderful magnifying glass for us.

It also did the job perfectly, zooming in on the little lava river. Within seconds we'd seen what we needed—beasts that looked like some kind of unholy blend of fire and crocodile pulled themselves along the river of molten rock, coming to shore for brief moments.

"Boss, I don't wanna fight one of those."

"Agreed."

"Very agreed," Isha chimed in.

With three for getting out of here and none against it, we moved to avoid the mountain altogether, pulling away, only to discover another the next day, and then another. Mountains were replaced by them one by one, and in no lesser number along the far edge of this strip of shore. I worried which was the one I was supposed to look at, a worry I need not have had.

CHAPTER 31

BIRTH OF FIRE

A black colossus crept slowly over the horizon, building and building until it stood tall above any and all around it. As we approached what could only be described as the nastiest-looking active volcano I had ever seen, I frowned. The sky was blackened by thick, burning rivers of soot—not the small streams that had flowed down its companions, but roiling tides of death. I could even see monsters from a few miles out flowing upon its surface, pulling themselves around the burning rock.

"Feels like someone's supposed to throw a ring into that," I mumbled.

"What?" Isha asked curiously.

"Nothing, but this is decidedly the one they want us checking on."

"You think?" Chien quipped. "Lens first?"

"Yeah, let's see what we can see before getting near it."

He pulled out his newest spell, and we saw that it was easily as much of a bleak hellscape as I'd feared. It looked like even the ground was steaming. That was probably as much as the elder had wanted, just confirming that there was nothing too odd going on, but it wasn't enough for me. If I was going to do a job, it would pay to do it right.

"All right, I've got something I'm going to try," I told them.

I'd played with the idea of flight and found it to be awful. Now I tried again, wrapping bands of force around me like ropes and pulling myself up. The sensation was awful, my inner ear screaming as my point of perception shifted along with where I was trying to move to, but I had an idea.

Once I was up I didn't simply try to move myself forward. Instead, I visualized something akin to a zip line and set it into the sky before me. Then I hooked my rope-like construct to it and tried pulling myself along. This, while still rather unpleasant, seemed to remove the worst of the nausea, rendering it a much smaller issue.

"You can fly?!" Isha asked. "Not even Elaya could do that!" she shouted, referencing the elder from the village we grew up in. She was right too. Flight was an obscenely rare skill.

"It sort of works. Okay, I'm gonna go and see what I can. I'll be back. Keep each other safe until I return."

"Be careful," Isha admonished as I flew away.

The path was halting, as I had to stop to make new lines to flow along, but it did function. My long and arduous practice making more and more physical forces helped too, making the whole thing easier. I loved that aspect of magic, that things we practiced got easier. Soon I was zooming along over the mountainside, looking at all the beasts below me.

Most of them seemed standard, something I'd seen from Chien's lens, but among them there were a few outliers. Bigger versions of the same type of monster curled up in some of the pools, the large reptilian lava-lizards seeming relaxed. In and of itself, that didn't seem a problem, but it was notable. I also saw them fighting each other, with a few situations where one ripped another to bits.

If I had to guess, these—or other related beasts—were what the northern elves hunted for their well-loved heating stones. Even if they weren't actively using magic, these beasts were clearly magical in nature, with black, cracked skin that showed fire leaking through beneath. I'd wager that within each was a stone like those I'd made, the size of a grain of sand or something similar.

Thankfully, there were no winged creatures flying around, nor any sign of anything that might nest and come for me. If I'd seen even one, I'd have turned back, unwilling to try fighting while flying. Too risky. So I continued on toward the top of the mountain.

Thick waterfalls of lava cascaded down the black cliffs, raining burning death upon the land below. I avoided them, going up and up, higher along the dark stone. They must have been falling from the bottom of the caldera, as the cliffs rose hundreds of feet higher above them.

As I crested the peak I looked down. The bowl inside had to be the size of a city, with rippling black and red soup bubbling and churning in the natural cauldron. The sides were high, high enough that after checking the heat of the rock, I was safe to land. The heat dissipated before reaching this altitude.

The beasts from below were absent here. Perhaps they needed a shore, something this caldera lacked, or perhaps some other quirk kept them away. No other monsters were roaming about either; however, that didn't mean that there was no sign of one.

A skeleton clung to the inside of the caldera, looking like some sort of T-rex, but larger—the size of a skyscraper. It was clearly long dead, bones peeking out beneath cracked and broken scales, thick as the armor on a tank. Below it the rock seemed to boil like water on a stove. Slowly, I guided myself over to the massive dead beast, careful to keep well away from the burning gasses and stone below.

With care I made it near one of the claws, the hands it had been using to try and hold on to the edge. The nails looked calcified, and the bones had layers of rock from old eruptions splattered upon it. Whatever this beast had been, it had found the slightest slope it could and lain down before its death, allowing the body to stay where it was, even as its tissues fell away. Certainly this thing must have died centuries ago, the heat and lack of any predators preserving it.

As I contemplated trying to get one of the armor plates, I looked at the lava below and realized I'd been wrong. I thought it was boiling as I approached, but that wasn't so. No. What appeared to be bubbles weren't bubbles at all. They were massive eggs, each the size of a school bus, and they floated atop the molten stone.

Curious, I made a lens like Chien had and looked down. Within each and every one I could see a creature like the one before me, only a fraction of the size. Was this normal? Did this thing naturally lay eggs here? How long until one hatched? Most of them had little monsters of black or red inside, but one of them was smaller, and inside was a creature of pure white. I looked down at it almost in pity. It must be a runt or have some defect.

While I was looking the membranes over, the unborn monster's eyelids pulled back, and a pitch-black eye looked up at me. I sucked in a breath, for I could feel a wave of visceral hate and anger in that eye, staring back into the lens I'd made, boring into my very soul. I dropped the spell and flew away. Internally, I knew it couldn't hurt me, but it still felt as if the beast could see me and wanted nothing more than to end my life.

Moments later, I returned to Chien and Isha, zooming back as quickly as I could. My hair stood on end, frayed from the mere seconds of looking at that little creature.

"Hey boss, everything good?" Chien asked as I landed near him.

"I think so, yeah," I said. "We should tell the villages that there are some large eggs up there, though. Nothing moving around yet, but they may want to keep an eye out."

"Is everything okay?" Isha asked.

"I think so."

Little did I know that at that moment a small horn was ripping through the membrane of an egg, releasing a monster unseen for generations.

CHAPTER 32

BREAK FOR FORGING

As with all things, travel down the coast took time. After passing the massive volcanic mountain of doom things slowly went back to some semblance of normalcy. I wondered if there was something like a ring of fire on this world, as there had been on Earth. If so, was it the mountain region I was so familiar with? I didn't think so, as none on the other side of the continent had had any signs of volcanic activity.

I thought about this as we made our way along the shore. At night we had to find somewhere safe from the menace that was the ocean, but that was easier than dealing with angry flaming mountains.

"What ya doing there, boss?" Chien asked as I walked along, one hand roving over the sands gently.

"Look," I said, showing him the handful of black sand.

"More iron?"

"We're almost out of trade goods, and a few tools wouldn't be bad either."

"Have to build a forge," he pointed out.

"You know, I don't know if we do. Between the two of us I'm pretty sure we could smelt it without one, but even if we do, we can improvise one pretty quickly."

"No other reasons you're doing that?" Isha chimed in, knowing me well.

"There are actually," I said. "I've been thinking."

"Dangerous," she said, getting a nod from our other companion.

"I've gotten good enough at fire and force magic that I can now make crystals of them. What if I could do the same with other basic forces? I could start building something bigger, more . . . lasting."

"She's right," Chien said with a shake of his head. "Dangerous."

I roved back to my thoughts. "I want a boat."

"Like the ones used to go down rivers?" Chien asked.

There were such things—canoes and rafts—basically used to move goods and people between cities, but they were painfully basic.

"Not quite. I want one good enough to go on the ocean."

"Saw a guy take a canoe out there once," Chien informed me, and that was news to me.

"How did it go?"

"Well enough until a wave hit it wrong and flipped the whole thing. Think we wanted a moving version of one or a fishing platform."

Platforms were easy enough for our people, and popular too. Basically just tied to trees or the like; with the ability of some elves to grow said trees into the perfect shape or in the perfect place, it made going up sensible. Once or twice I'd even seen people primarily weave them from vines, but that was a lot more work.

"So, how do you think we should go about building a boat for the ocean?" Isha asked, seeming almost curious.

"No idea." That got me a pair of guffaws, as normally I had at least some vague notion.

I did have some thoughts. I mean, I understood how boats worked. Water displacement was easy enough to wrap my head around and could lead to really interesting designs. However, that didn't mean I knew anything at all about building a boat. Even with my perfect memory, even with all the times I'd seen things and watched videos and the like, I was drawing nearly a complete blank. Boatbuilding was something that had never really caught my interest, and I knew enough to know it wasn't a simple subject.

"So you want something you have no idea how to make? That might be a first," Isha laughed.

"Definitely a first," Chien agreed.

"Both of you shut up. I don't know everything."

"But you know a lot of things," Chien pointed out.

"Sure, a lot of things."

They kept on for most of the rest of the day. By that point, I was very thoroughly decided that I was going to have to build not only one, but many boats. There would be no other way to wipe this particular failing off of my record. If I didn't, they'd probably pester me for the next century or two.

That thought brought a smile to my face as I laid down to sleep. No longer did I have the gnawing fear of old age, of people leaving me like they did before. My family could live on forever, or almost forever, so long as they weren't killed. I'd lost loved ones in both lives, but in my first so many had fallen to the specter of age. Once I brought this world forward, we could have entire cities filled with ancients, and we could tame the world together as one. That dream carried me through the night.

The mountains went back to being just that, mountains, and as we moved, they slowly retreated from the shore. It still wasn't anything like a wide opening, with the sentinels maintaining their vigil in the far distance, but it was noticeable.

We stopped for a few days at that point, taking the time to build a more secure structure and forge out the iron I'd gathered. There was no hurry. Even if we wanted this mission to be over, there wasn't any reason we had to keep moving, and the weather was nice. So, a vacation was called for. Also, the sled was getting heavy with all the ore I was building up in it.

"This seemed easier when we did it back home," Chien said as we poured our first ingot.

"Because we had a whole shop full of tools. I assure you it was this hard at first."

We managed to forge out a small stump anvil, a little contraption that fit into said stump, and a matching hammer. It wasn't big, but big enough for some simple work. This was followed by a set of knives. Knives were too useful to not have, and somewhere through the trading we'd lost one. They were poor compared to my normal work, but still ages above what most people had—just simple iron blades.

The few days of work were followed by a full week of rest, during which Isha began working with plants. She didn't say anything, but I saw her once or twice out of the corner of my eye. Perhaps she was working on something special, and if so, I relished the chance at a surprise.

Chien and I took apart the forge with all the gusto of two young men who had a chance to destroy something, and we set off, eager to get to our next destination.

CHAPTER 33

LAST STOP BEFORE THE BOG

Sometimes it seemed like this journey would never end. Days upon days passed, and though I missed the comfort of being at home and the friends I'd left there, I didn't hate where I'd ended up. We picked our way south, slowly advancing after our short break.

What we eventually came upon was a proper town, not some small village. It stood at the mouth of a great river, between the forest and a massive saltwater marsh. People were going about their days and looked at us strangely as we approached, like they'd never seen anyone not from here before. None approached, though, and being that we had business, we didn't bother them either.

We approached the wall, a small fortification that circled the hill the town had been built upon, grown from briars and trees. There were people nestled above them somehow, atop some kind of platform or similar, allowing them to look out over the landscape, but there weren't many. There were also none at the gates, though more and more people began to give us looks.

"We're getting a lot of attention," Isha whispered to me.

"I don't think they get many visitors," I said. "Luckily, they don't seem to object to us, just curious I think."

People were everywhere, and if I estimated correctly, this place had several hundred residents. That alone was a good sign, though an odd one, since most of the villages we'd passed had at most a couple dozen. It also meant that whoever was in charge here would be slightly more entrenched, and with the setup, I didn't doubt that they had more experience than the average village leader.

There were also no obvious shops, though with a community this size, would there really need to be any? If only a handful of people made or performed any given service, they'd just be known, and you could go to their homes for what you needed. That was tiresome, but not completely unexpected, as most villages were the same, but it did mean no inns or the like.

I wondered if we'd need to find the local leader, but of course, that worry was worthless, because he found us.

"Greetings, strangers," came the voice from off to our side.

"Good day, elder," I said as we turned toward him.

The elf in question was clearly older, half his hair white and eyes that showed almost a tiredness from his years, but he still smiled.

"Welcome to my town," he said. "It is seldom that we get visitors from afar."

"Afar?" asked Chien.

"Your skin and style are too different from our own to be from either our north or south. You aren't pale like those from the matriarch's home; nor do you have the clothes of the swamps. Not that many of either make it to this edge of the world. Where are my manners, though? My name is Lokan, a pleasure to meet you."

We quickly gave our names and offered one of the knives Chien and I had made. It was poorer than most of our work, but an iron knife was still far and above what most people in this world had.

"A wonderful gift. Allow me to return the favor—you should stay with me for the night, as my home has the most room."

It was no secret that it would also allow him to keep an eye on us and prevent any trouble from brewing, but that was fine since we needed to speak to him anyway.

He led us to his home, where he had several servants—they were marked up like those in Atal to note how many years were left on their time—and excused himself. Regardless of where they were, administrators were always busy.

As for the room itself, it was cozy, if basic. In the center was a fire pit lined with stones, and a large sleeping area filled with soft grasses and the like lay off to one side. It almost reminded me of my first home, though the building was stronger than that hut had been.

We were invited to dinner, a large affair where all the people of the house sat around sharing the massive quantity of food. As guests, we were sat beside Lokan and his family so we could talk.

"I was asked to check on the one mountain on the way here," I began.

"Were you? I appreciate that, since our hunters seldom get close to it."

"Yes, there's a large skeleton there, and . . ." I wasn't sure how to phrase it so it didn't sound overly alarming. ". . . a large number of eggs."

The elder sat back, his eyes widening slightly. "My, you got close indeed to have seen that."

"I don't know if you need to send someone . . ."

"I don't," he replied. "Those have been there since before I was born and will likely be there well into the future. The bones you saw belonged to the beast whose heart now heats Icehome, supposedly slain by old Neera." He leaned in close, as if sharing a conspiratorial secret and continued, "I suspect she merely found the beast dead or injured after laying those eggs and harvested its heart."

"Good to know that it's not a worry then."

"None at all, my young friend."

"Would you mind if I asked you a few questions?"

"Of course not, go on."

"The elders in our area didn't know anything about the situation in the swamps—if there was an ancient ruling them, or what had happened. Could you clarify who's in charge for me?"

"No." I must have shown how taken aback I was on my face because he continued. "It isn't that I don't want to, Justin, but that I cannot. We get visitors from the villages just to our north every now and then—one or two a year perhaps—but from the south? It has been over a century since any have come this way. That last one was to tell us their previous leader had died, much like your own message."

"Are they so insular? Do they not send out any traders at all?" I asked, stunned at the lack of communication.

"You've never been to the swamps have you?" he asked, amused.

"No . . ."

"Then you haven't a clue of the scale. First of all, most of it is devoid of our people. Nobody likes living in a bog. Well, almost nobody. So, the majority of it is just open land." He reached down in the dirt and began to draw a map as he spoke.

"I see."

"You're from Atal, right?" At my nod, he added that to the map, making a line upward. "You must have traveled north and around, through the forests, and the ice."

There was a sense of scale to his map as he proceeded. Our lands were medium sized, but as he moved northward he showed the enormity of the frozen wastes. Then he moved downward, adding mountains and the slim strip of coast we were on now. From his drawing, I could see that the lands within the circling mountains that had previously belonged to the ancient Cino were quite a bit larger than the forests of my birth.

"And the swamps?" I asked.

"Down here. Most of the people live around a large inland sea, bigger than any lake upon a series of three great hills. Those aren't as tall as our mountains, supposedly, but high enough to avoid the waters. Here and there within the swamp are other settlements, places where the land is dry enough to make small woodlands, but most of it is home to nothing but beasts, bugs, and those who would rather be left alone." As he spoke he drew and pointed out the structures he mentioned.

The swamp we were looking at wasn't some small thing. It was massive, almost as large as the ice shelf. I could also imagine the "joy" of crossing such a thing and frowned. The lake he spoke of, and the hills where we were likely to find whatever leader there may be, were also at the very point of the map.

"What you thinking, boss?" Chien asked, leaning in.

"We're gonna need a better way to travel."

CHAPTER 34

I'M RUBBER

We decided to stay in the town a bit longer than we'd originally intended. I wanted a better way to cross the divide before setting off—even an imperfect one—to reduce our travel time. I didn't delude myself either. There was no way this was going to get us all the way, but even partway would be a boon.

An airboat would've been the perfect thing, but sadly that was probably impossible. There were other options, though. We could try making something seaworthy and sailing around, but I knew there were monsters in the sea and didn't know how to make anything even remotely seaworthy. Canoes were another good option, giving us at least the option to skip the mud.

"What about using the shore like we have been?" Chien suggested as I bounced ideas off of him.

"Might work for parts of it, but I've been told there are a lot of swampy seaside areas once you get a day or two down the coast. And, that wouldn't solve our trouble getting further inland to find those cities."

"Shame we can't all just fly."

Now that was an idea . . . Planes were beyond our capability at the moment, but what if we could fly? Could a glider be made? Probably not. I needed something simpler in the whole building department. Something easier, less joints. If we had enough fabric, a hot air balloon would be perfect.

"If only we had something that could hold air," I moped.

"Don't know something like that," Chien said. "Ask the locals, maybe?"

"Good call," I said, praising him for the advice. There were still a lot of things I didn't know.

As I walked around town asking questions, I thought about other options. Carbon fiber sounded cool, and might be light enough to work, but I didn't know how to make it. Cloth just wasn't available, at least not the quality and types we'd need for something like this. Leather? No, leather was far too heavy, even at its thinnest, and who knew if I could even get that. What about leaves or something then, or growing one? No, somehow I doubted that would be possible.

"Actually, I do know of something," one of the townsfolk said.

"Do tell," I answered with a smile and a nod.

"There's a tree just on the edge of the swamp," he said. "The inner bark is pretty light, and you can get huge sheets of it. It should hold air too. It's all weird feeling, like soft skin."

I was over the moon. Hot air balloons, here I come! He even took the time to show me. All he asked for in return was to help him cut some of the wood for his own purposes, something I could do in seconds. A deal struck, we headed out of town and toward the edge of the marsh.

The trees we were looking for weren't uncommon, but I had a feeling nobody really thought about them holding air, so nobody took to them the way I was now. Each was wide and squat, with a look that almost reminded me of cypress otherwise.

"These them?" I asked my guide.

"Indeed," he said. "Just need to cut it down and strip the limbs, and we can get the bark for you. This makes great firewood too!" He hefted his ax, having brought it along. I didn't bring any such thing, but I assumed he wanted to trade off. That didn't work for me.

With a quick series of hand motions, a series of sharp cuts were made into the lumber. My guide stood back, sputtering as I felled a tree within seconds, which would've taken an hour or so by hand. Kinetics was one of my favorites, and so it was no issue to slice where I wanted, though, I could tell that this tree was significantly more durable than most I'd run into. Next came the limbs, sliced away and piled to the side.

"Well . . . that's one way to do it. Er, how close did you say you were to becoming an elder?"

"Not at all. Now, for the inner bark. Can I just slice along the length and peel it like a fruit?"

"Yeah, that would work." The man was still stunned by the quick work, answering almost in autopilot. The outer bark cracked and fell away, leaving a long sheet of brilliant orange. Just from the cuts I'd made alone, I could tell the stuff was tough enough for my needs. I smiled, until I tried to pick it up.

"Something wrong?" he asked nervously.

"I thought you said this was light?"

"It's very light for something that keeps air out, and I know it does too. I've seen bubbles get trapped in it before."

The sheet in my hand was about a quarter inch thick, but rather than canvas or nylon, it was like rubber, thick rubber. The consistency wasn't quite the same—it had a grainy feel to it—but rubber was the closest thing I could compare it to. Even if I sliced it into thinner sheets, I doubted it would make good material for balloons.

"I, uh, don't suppose you'd help me get some of this back to town?" the would-be woodsman asked hesitantly.

Technically, I'd more than fulfilled my end of our bargain, but goodwill was worth the effort, and getting it back if you lost it wasn't easy. If I told him to kick sand, he wouldn't be able to complain that I'd reneged on our deal, but I knew he'd also never help me again, and some of the people in town might not either. Small towns were rumor mills, and I was decidedly an outsider. Maybe I wasn't planning to return, but our kind had long memories.

"Well, you helped me out, so I can help a little, but this is a lot, even for me. I won't be able to get all of it all the way there."

"Can you get the main trunk back?"

"I can do that."

It was a sizable tree, and even if I wasn't taking it all, getting this much back was no easy task. Several breaks were taken throughout the day, and it occurred to me that had I not been here, this would be a task for a good few men. Well, either that or my companion would've had to make a lot of runs back and forth. It also wasn't lost on me that he didn't want the tree cut into more manageable lengths. Perhaps at the beginning he'd been thinking of firewood, but with it whole, he could hew planks from it—a much more valuable use for any wood.

When I finally made it back to our rooms, Isha looked at me with a raised brow. I'd not been planning to be gone the whole day.

In response, I hauled the tied-up roll of rubber-like bark over my shoulder and before me, where it sort of bounced up and down like rubber was keen to do.

"I swear, you do the weirdest things."

CHAPTER 35

BOUNCY!

Why, why would you get this stuff?!" Chien fumed, trying to cut the sheet of rubber back.

"Goodness," I said, "Use magic. This stuff isn't that bad." I, of course, was using only magic because it was in fact that bad. The material was like trying to cut through wood, which made sense, since it was bark.

"Do you even know how to use it?"

"I've got a few ideas."

He made a chopping motion, sending a magical blade to slice off the strip he was trying to cut. "Ideas, he says . . ."

"We can probably sew it together."

"No," Isha said from a corner, where she was prepping some plants for dinner. "Not unless you're doing it, because I don't have a needle that will go through that, and you're not ruining one of my good ones. A thick iron one maybe, but that seems nonsensical."

"Well, maybe it melts."

"Will it remain waterproof afterward? And even if it does, this stuff is heavy." Chien had spotted the same problem I had.

"Sure, but we can make a boat out of it, maybe one to go along the top of the marsh."

I'd written off airboats, but if we worked it right, this stuff might just work for a raft that we could then push like we had the sled. Well, at least that was the best I was coming up with, unless someone had a bunch of helium sitting around, and even that would be iffy.

"Changing the plan again then, Justin?" Isha teased.

"He does do that a lot."

"Enough, both of you. We have to work with what we have, unless you want to spend the next couple of years trudging through bug- and monster-infested mud."

"..."

"..."

"That's what I thought."

"Do we have to go, though?" Isha asked.

"What do you mean?"

"I mean, we could just go home. Nobody knows if there even is an ancient in the swamps, and they never talk to anyone anyways. Or we could stay here. It's fairly nice, Justin. It would be easy. Is there really anything back there other than a few friends? And we could just wait a while and go home later too."

I looked at her, and I could see it in her eyes. She was tired. We all were; we just wanted to go home. Sure, I knew that we might find some trouble on this journey, but nothing like the environments we had. They probably didn't know how to parse the tundra we'd been through, or the rivers of lava. Anyone else might have just called it and packed up, but I had a stubborn streak a mile wide.

"We could," I said, "but we're so close, I just want to finish right."

"All right, but you're going to owe me something when it's all over."

"Sure, name it."

"I'll tell you later," she said with a mischievous grin before taking her work and leaving us.

"I'm with you 'til the end, boss," Chien told me, shrugging, once she'd left.

"Oh? No demands?"

He tapped his chin for a minute. "When you take over, I want to be in charge of the treasury."

I raised an eyebrow at him. "Assuming I do."

"You will, boss, one day." He said it without the smallest hint of doubt, like it was just a fact, the truth.

"Fine, you can be minister of finance when I rule Atal. Now let's get back to this." I really didn't want to argue with him about the fact that I never wanted to rule anything, so I just pointed to our project.

The rubber—I was simply going to call it that—did in fact melt. It got to a pretty good temperature, not forge hot, but fire hot, so I wasn't worried about it doing so in the short term. Even once that was done, the seams weren't perfect, and were very prone to breaking from each other. The stuff was at least still tough everywhere except the joints, enough that it took a sharp knife and a lot of purely magical effort to slice it up.

Since just melting had failed, we went for a series of connections. Sewing it first didn't seem to solve everything, after taking a day to make the needle we needed and some thick twine. The next one involved sewing a reinforcement strip over every joint and melting it all. The joined pieces were huge too. Since we'd just cut the tree-sized strip in half and sewn the edges, it was about fifteen-feet wide and just as long. They were monstrous trees, but the joint looked good.

"Think it'll hold?" my assistant asked, smacking the bouncy surface.

"Have to test it."

"We're gonna be going over dirt and water fast, if what you're saying is true. How do we even test it, hold it out and slam something on it for a few hours?" he quipped.

I chuckled under my breath. "Yes, that's exactly what we're gonna do. Can you gather up the kids from the town? Maybe the adults too, since it's getting later in the day. I bet they're all done with their work for today."

"And bring them here?" he asked, looking around the small, old hut that we'd managed to barter for access. The village elder had offered to keep hosting us, but it felt wrong if we were going to be here for a couple of weeks.

"No, just outside the village, by the nearest trees. Get Isha too, wherever she's run off to." I didn't look back as I grabbed some rope and hauled off the huge rubber tarp.

I found the perfect spot in minutes—several trees with a nice big opening between them, nothing too sharp nearby, soft grass and mud below it, and easy to see from the village. Preparing was simple enough—a few holes, a few ropes. The fact that I had no springs would make this passable at best, but it would still be fun.

"Hey . . . We need to . . . test how strong this is! . . . Want to help?" I said between jumps at the approaching group of elves. They all thought we were weird, but we traded well, and they seemed to think anything we wanted to show them might be neat.

"He is such a child sometimes," I heard Isha whisper as I tried to get higher and higher on this world's first trampoline. She still joined me, though.

The village's children, what few there were, showed their emphatic agreement by bouncing on moments later. The adults gave them a bit of time before switching out, letting the little ones tire themselves out. This continued well into the night, with some of those capable of magic sending up lights and food appearing from somewhere. It was fun, and by the end of it, I was satisfied that our material would hold up.

CHAPTER 36

AN AGREEMENT

After a long evening of bouncing up and down—pun decid-edly intended—we retired. The rubber had held up admira-bly, without any visible damage of note. As people left I inspected it, and it seemed that the extra reinforcement had done its job perfectly. Sure, there were one or two small deformations, but I couldn't even find any cracks in it, so I called it a resounding success.

There were a number of ways I could have gone about building a boat, with designs and plans that might have worked, but there was only one that I strongly considered. A basic raft shape should work. It wouldn't be super efficient or ideal for any given circumstance, but it should function. Sometimes you simply had to do what would serve now and not worry about what might serve later.

Building a basic frame was easy enough, if only because of the massive amount of wood Chien and I needed to harvest for the bark. It seemed wasteful, but once we left it could serve as firewood for this little town or building materials. I didn't really care. The townsfolk did give us odd looks, though, as we brought back tree after tree.

"We don't have to bring all of these back, boss," he said one day. "It's not like we need them all."

"We're taking the trees down one way or another," I'd replied. "No need to make waste."

"I suppose."

From there, everything was fairly straightforward. The thickest sheets of the rubber bark were used as the base, though the addition was minimal. Thinner sheets served for the sides in the form of tubes, though I was making the bottom slightly inflated too, for added comfort. The real issue was getting it all together and done properly.

Our raft was about fifteen feet long and about eight wide, and while that might seem large, it would decidedly limit the places we could go, and it would also be serving as our shelter in case of storm. It was a small rig, so the thinnest sheets of rubber we could find would serve as a tarp to go over it and we'd be dry. Though netting was impossible, sadly, we could at least keep rain away. The different parts would all be sealed together, but not connected internally, so they might be replaced if needed. There would also be plenty of room for our stuff, as even compacted, we'd gathered a fair amount on the sleds over the course of our trip.

It took us a full week to gather all the rubber we thought we needed, and another to get the design laid out over some logs that would serve as the frame. A third week to get more rubber, since we'd underestimated the amount we'd need significantly. That's when we ran into a problem.

"How's that supposed to keep its shape?" Isha asked as she watched us pull the frame out. The tube instantly collapsed into a floppy mess.

"We'll fill them with air," I said confidently, and then I realized my issue.

"How? And how will that help?" she asked, only to see me sigh.

"Don't worry," Chien said confidently. "The boss has got this."

There was no pump, and even if there was, we didn't have a proper valve. I'd love to say that I could just build one, but I really couldn't. I had no clue how the valves on inflatable rafts and what-not worked. I could picture one, sure. I'd even used a ton of them in my former life, but I'd never tried to figure out how they functioned.

As was my normal solution, when my knowledge failed, I fell upon my magic. We already had bellows from our earlier forging that wouldn't do well for a pump, and we were already sealing it, leaving only one small opening for the end because of how we had to sew these together. Making a one-way barrier was weird, though; unintuitive.

It took a full day for me to get it because there were so many moving parts. I needed an opening that would let air in, but not out, that would let the tip of the bellows in and out, and could be held for a long period. Several times we made it about halfway where it needed to be, only for my control to slip, the whole thing releasing air in an infuriating sound that resembled a whoopee cushion, which was fitting, I supposed.

Finally, we did it, and Chien rushed to get the last hole sealed up. It would be the weakest point, but with both the sewing and the heat treatment, I felt it should hold.

"Let's never do this again," he said when we were finally done, leaning back against it. "Good pillow, though."

"Chien, that was just one side. We've still got the other, the back, and the floor to go."

"Fuck," he grumbled, in English. He'd heard me say it one too many times over the course of our years-long association. There was a similar word in the local elven dialects, but it didn't have the broad use, or the good hearty power, of an old-fashioned *fuck*.

The rest of the work was easier, taking us only another day. I'd have liked to have had more air pressure, but there was only so much I could justify fighting. At the end of the day, Isha and I laid in it, looking up at the stars as we rested on some light furs.

"This is comfy," she said as she snuggled up to me. "Why did you never make something like this before?"

"Never really occurred to me."

"Well, when we get back, I want something like this for our bed."

"I'll see what I can do. Glad that you decided you're happy to continue."

"Oh, I'm not happy," she said, moving to straddle my stomach. "I've made friends here. We could still stay." She must have been able to see my face because she leaned down. "But I can see you don't want to, so I'll go."

I'd not really been paying proper attention to her, or I would have known she'd been making friends. Chien and I always kept people at arm's length, but with weeks here it seemed Isha had made connections.

"Thank you," I muttered.

"Oh, you don't have to thank me. I told you already there'd be a price." Her voice was mischievous, and I could see her teeth as she smiled.

"And what's that?" I asked, holding her close.

"You're taking a break from all your wild adventures—no wars, no wandering about the world, none of that nonsense."

"It's not like I want to . . ."

"You could have told them to shove it, but you didn't. You will in the future, until your break is over." Her voice was hard.

"All right then, and how long a break will this be?" I asked her.

"Until our first child is grown," she declared, fingers entwining with mine.

"I think I can do that."

Upon reflection, I had to agree. Something like this raft would make an excellent bed.

CHAPTER 37

FIRST NIGHT IN THE SWAMP

Leaving the village was actually a bit of an event. It wasn't something we'd planned, but it seemed with the few visitors they'd received, and the fact that we'd stayed long enough for Isha to make a few friends, people had come to find us fun. Though introducing a new game for the kids had also endeared me to them somewhat.

Well-wishers came to see us off as we carried the raft from town, a few walking with us down the street, the crowd growing. The children were looking for something interesting, the women chatting with Isha. Even the local elder looked amused as he watched on.

"Bye, everyone," we said as we threw the little boat into the river that separated this area from the swamp. "See you!"

The first few moments in the water were anticlimactic, being as we weren't going all that fast. Then the spells I was planning to use fell into place. The boat began to move forward over the murky water, faster and faster until we were bouncing lightly over the gunk.

Soon enough we were really going, and we all began to catch some air. Each time we went over something we went up and were thrown about.

"We really need tie-downs!" Chien said as he hit the floor hard. Before he could bounce upward again, I saw him spin out a spell. Thin ropes of force began to tie us all in place.

"Thank you!" Isha said as she tried to hold herself in place, white-knuckling the straps on our gear.

"Maybe we should slow down . . ." As I spoke I pulled back on the speed a little. ". . . and I'm not sure about tie-downs; there are ups and downs."

Sure, it would be nice to have something to hold me in place, but what if the boat flipped? That could be really dangerous. Maybe we could do some for the gear and then bury ourselves in it? I didn't know yet. It was something to think about. I wondered if I could even add something like that right now without reconstructing large parts of the boat.

"We're making decent time," Isha said as she looked back at the few people on shore who were now fading from sight. Walking this would have taken us hours.

"Hmm, some way to keep it going without effort on my side too," I mused.

My thoughts went back to some of my projects before the war in Atal really took all of my time. In my first life, I'd been designing computers, and now I had the time to make one of pure magic. With the crystallized magic I could create, something truly neat would be possible. I might even be able to make it capable of imparting some effects to make things happen in reality.

While I was getting deeper into the weeds on those thoughts Chien shouted.

"BUMP!" It seemed that while I was distracted I'd missed a little spit of land, tossing us all into the air as I steered us at it. Perhaps it would be better to pay attention to what I was doing now.

"Er, sorry," I said as Isha turned to glare at me.

For the next few hours we just plodded along at moderate speed, until my mana started to get low. Chien was less interested in speed than I was, so while I got comfy and rested, he had us floating at a slow clip. It meant that I didn't need to do as he had and keep us all secured, which was nice, but I also liked going quick.

Even though we set out near dawn, we weren't expecting to see anything for a long time. So, as the large fiery orb began to sink into the horizon, we looked for a place to park.

"So, land?" Chien asked.

"Might be better in case there's rain, but I don't know that we really need it. The bottom of this thing is thick enough that it'll be fine if we sit on the water too." I started to get the top set up, since we wouldn't want to be exposed to the air while we rested. I could only shudder at the thought of what kind of insects lived in a swamp like this.

I realized how dense I was as I put the roof on. We already had a few spots where things could be secured, kept from flopping everywhere. Tomorrow I'd see if we could set up something, but for tonight we just needed to rest.

As Chien pulled onto a little muddy island in the middle of the water, I shut everything up, sealing the boat from the outside world, just as dark truly began to fall. We could still hear the outside—birds chirping, splashes every now and then, a fish jumping around in the water, and the wind in the trees. It was pleasant, and something I'd much gotten used to in this life—sleeping to the sounds of nature.

Isha and I curled up on one side of the craft, and Chien took the other. We talked briefly about the day, about what had worked, what hadn't, and where we could improve. Before long, we all started to drift off. After all, it had been a long day.

"Hey, boss!" came a slightly worried call in the middle of the night.

"Problem?" I asked, sitting up quickly and trying to spin some combat magic into place. There were few reasons to wake me, and none of them good.

"Maybe?" he sounded unsure.

I quickly joined him at the slightly open door where he stood. The little ball of light he'd made hovered over the swamp, reflected in dozens of eyes. The creatures themselves looked rather like gators, though wider than any I'd ever seen, and stood slightly higher up off the ground. They were still large reptiles, though, and none were attacking.

"I just got up to go relieve myself and . . ."

"Yeah, we might not be doing that outside at night. May need to set something up for the day too. Anyway, they don't seem to be aggressive, so for now we can just keep to ourselves."

"I still gotta pee," he said.

"Need a chamber pot . . . or a bag, I guess . . ." We had the materials so making one in the morning wouldn't be a problem.

"Fine, I'll figure something out."

I tried, and failed, to get back to sleep. The number of predators was bugging me. Animals on this world were far more aggressive than those on Earth. It made sense, though. Back on Earth, humans had been at the tippy top of the food chain, feared by everything that had survived our ascent—or rather only the things that had feared us had survived our ascent. Here, though, plenty of things could get away with eating elves now and then, and many did. So few of the animals in this world feared us.

After an hour or two of failed sleep, I grumbled and got back up. Chien was there too, looking at the doors.

"You can rest if you like," I told him. "I'll keep a watch." Watch was another thing I'd hoped to avoid with the larger raft, but it seemed we wouldn't be able to.

"If I could, I would," he said. "Don't think I'll get a wink for the rest of the night."

I smiled. More of my English was rubbing off on him.

CHAPTER 38

TURTLE

It didn't take long for us to come to a tenuous peace with the environment. The gators were the largest predators around, and since they were content to do nothing but stare at us, everything else followed their lead. And man, were there a lot of animals.

The islands we encountered had small bugs that kept well away from the water but seemed to rip around on any of the roots they could find. The other animals, namely the pigs, were fairly normal looking too—not unusual, not magical or mutated at all—just pigs. That was nice. Actually, it was amazing, since I knew a good few recipes for pork that I loved and hadn't been able to make for quite some time. Not sure where I was going to find vinegar, but if I could, we could all be rolling in pulled pork.

Other animals were also similar to the ones on Earth. Large birds, snakes, and even some fish, and nothing obviously magical. I wondered briefly if that was good or bad for this world, but then again, magical animals weren't exactly common anywhere. There was also a distinct lack of mosquitoes—a blessing from whatever power had brought me to this world. On the other hand, there were plenty of biting flies, but those were easier to deal with.

"I know that look; what are you thinking?" Isha asked as I reflected on this about a week into our journey.

"This place is rather peaceful compared to the last few we've been to."

"Speak for yourself," Chien griped. Several of the biting flies had feasted on him.

"Devoid of . . ." As I spoke there was a roar. It seemed our little boat had run over one of the gators. ". . . actually dangerous animals." This was neither the first, nor would it be the last, time we'd hit one of them.

"I'd rather not tangle with one of those," Isha said as the creature tried, and failed, to follow us.

"Eh, we've seen worse." It was true. Those things would've been considered a problem back on Earth, but in this world? They were nothing like those to us.

"Better than the damn ice birds," Chien said with a shudder. Having to run in the middle of our night had been awful. Both Isha and I nodded in agreement.

"There's something ahead," Isha said, pointing.

I'd missed it, but out of the trees and off to our side was a small rise sticking up out of the swamp, a large rounded hill. Oddly round, like almost perfectly symmetrical, and devoid of anything other than a small layer of moss upon it. I would've guessed it was maybe fifty feet end to end, sticking out of the muck by about ten feet, and easily the largest spit of land we'd seen.

"That looks sort of . . ." A beaked head popped up from the water and I banked away. "Like something we want nothing to do with!"

I had been wrong, thinking we were the apex predator of this swamp, and now the true king showed himself, or herself.

"A turtle?!" Chien asked, grabbing on as I cranked our speed to the maximum that I felt comfortable with.

"A SNAPPING TURTLE!" I yelled as the creature turned and began to chase us.

"Snapping?!" Isha cried in confusion.

She was just in time to see said giant turtle snap, its head shooting forward like a rocket and grabbing one of the gators we'd passed. The poor creature had no chance, head and tail flying as the larger beast clacked its mouth shut upon it. It didn't stop, though. It didn't even pause as it gulped down one of the beasts that had stressed out Chien just the night before.

A few moments later it snapped at us again, head thrusting at our boat, just a little too high. I was near the back, but so was Isha, and a few strands of her long hair ended up brushed by the beast's beak as we pulled away, sending her jumping back away from it.

Something about that pulled on my emotions like a finger on a harp, stressed until it snapped and sent a wave of fury through me. This overgrown bowl of soup had chased us, had scared us, had gotten a meal already, but it wanted more. Well, if it wanted more, then it was only proper it got some.

"Chien, get the boat, fast as you can." He was quick, and I felt his magic wrap the vessel and pull it in less than a second.

As soon as he was in control I leapt upward. Flying was still weird, the visualization of it still strange and disorienting, but I didn't need to be that accurate. After all, this thing was huge, and I was just getting on its back. I heard a gasp of surprise as I took off and another as I landed behind the turtle's head, high up on the shell.

Many people thought of fury like a fire, and in some cases that could be true. Rage could burn, smolder, and blaze, but it could also be cold as ice. I was used to fire as well, but it felt wrong here, failing, so I took a different approach. I slammed my open palm onto the shell of the beast and began to cast.

Fire was energy, pure and simple vibrations. Perhaps that was why I did so well with it. Perhaps it matched well with my thoughts on kinetic energy, my other favorite spell, but there was another direction too, wasn't there? Rather than tell the creature's flesh to vibrate, I commanded it to stop, to stay where it was and move no further.

There was less resistance than I would have expected. All creatures imbued with the power of magic had some innate protection against its effects. This could be minor, or major, or anywhere in between, but they would resist it. Even the weakest of magical beasts would be able to fight against some spells, but this thing had none of that. Perhaps it was because it relied on its shell—no doubt a powerful defense—instead of the innate aura that others focused on. I didn't know, but I was happy to take advantage of the fact.

I sent a wave of cold down several feet into the beast's body, spreading out like the roots of a tree. Around me frost cracked and blossomed along the shell, forming fractals and sparkling patterns in the algae and moss that had made a home upon this monster. It was so easy, so simple, to send the energy like a spear deep into the turtle's body, ruining flesh and blood as it moved, making razor-sharp crystals tear and rip into flesh that had no protections against it.

The creature made a sound not unlike a scream and tried to stop its momentum forward, pulling into its shell and trying to curl up against the attack. That didn't help, though. It wasn't some tooth penetrating it, but shards of ice, shards that broke as the monster's powerful muscles contracted and pulled it inward, sending spears of frozen water through even more flesh, lancing like needles for precious seconds.

It wouldn't be fatal, at least not immediately. If nothing else, this thing was big, and I was pretty sure that I'd missed any of the organs that kept it going. However, I had a feeling our cold-blooded foe wouldn't be chasing anything and had learned a valuable lesson about messing with boats. That was enough for now, so I ripped my hand away, leaving a layer of skin behind, and flew forward to catch up with my boat.

CHAPTER 39

MYSTERY

We didn't run into any other turtles quite the size of the first. After all, a predator of that magnitude cleared an area around themselves. We did encounter several smaller versions, half or less the size, but still dangerous. These we sent away with a barrage of cold, something they both understood and disliked. A cold-blooded animal, such as a turtle, couldn't really function if its body temperature dropped too much.

With magic being real, there was a good chance that there was a bigger turtle still, one on whose back we lived. I personally doubted it, but it would be ironic if we indeed lived on such a creature. Perhaps one day I'd figure out both a camera and a way to get it high enough to look. A joke like that could take centuries to make come to pass, though, so I wasn't holding my breath.

It wasn't until the first month into our journey that we saw our first sign of people, which was saying something, as we were moving at a rapid clip. There were buildings ahead, but no movement among them, no people going to and fro. The three of us shared a look of concern as we approached, for this was certainly not normal. In nearly every village we'd found so far there were people around, spotters that picked us out well before we made it to the village proper.

The village itself was seated upon a hill above the waters, two long, almost sandbar-like protrusions sticking out and meeting at a wide angle. There was a small outcropping, almost like a dock with trees molded to stick out where boats might land, but there were no boats. Small bays lay barren where people could have brought canoes or other small vessels.

We pulled up alongside it, the front of our raft bouncing against the clearly unnatural trees as we tied off with some vines.

"Where is everyone?" Chien asked.

"I don't know," I replied, "but something's up. Stick together, and keep your eyes open for danger."

With careful steps we moved toward the nearest structure, a small hut. There was no door. In most places that was normal enough, but what we found inside wasn't. The beds were still in place, though clearly rotting, their boughs and leaves used as mattresses old, weeks, perhaps months gone. A few poorly made baskets were lying around, as well as tools of much the same, but older, more worn ones.

Finding nothing of note, we moved on from the hut, and each house was the same, devoid of people, abandoned some time ago. Everything was arranged in a circle, and that was the only reason I didn't fall into the central fire pit. This place was organized much like my home village had been, with houses grouped around a large area for fires and sitting, shared meals, and stories.

"Justin?" Isha asked as she saw me looking at the fire pit. Plants had grown into the little hole in the ground, leaving the stones covered with leaves.

"Let's finish looking around, then we'll talk."

I'd calmed a bit. As long as we didn't see any trees with Croatoan written on them I figured I'd remain that way.

"This place is creeping me out," Chien said after we'd finished surveying the place. He'd been silent for most of the time, looking around, startled.

"What do you see?" I asked.

"Empty houses, abandoned it looks like," he said, and Isha nodded along.

"I don't like it," she added.

"What don't you see?" When both of them looked at me with confusion, I added, "No food, no bodies. All the tools look like old ones, not the favorites of whoever made them, no toys for children, no boats either. Haven't even seen a sign of fighting."

"You think they went on their own?" Isha asked.

"Yes, but why? The land here doesn't look too different from what we've seen elsewhere. There's plenty of game to hunt, and while I don't really know the plants they would be eating, I'd guess there's enough of those too." My companions nodded, seeming uncomfortable.

"They're probably the furthest out, right?" Chien asked.

"Pretty much," I agreed.

"Well, then maybe they pulled in for some reason. If a better spot opened up, they could have. And the coastal villages said they hadn't seen anyone in forever."

"But that wasn't odd either," Isha pointed out.

"We'll have to wait until we see the next village," I said. "If there's another somewhere around, they'd know."

Agreeing, we set back off. There was no real reason to stay here.

One large bonus to this place, though, was that there were clear inroads and outroads, places where the water was just a bit deeper, the path through the swamps a bit wider. It pointed us in at least the right direction if we were heading deeper in.

By following those paths, and with a bit of luck, we found another village two weeks later. However, it was the same as the first—empty and long abandoned. A week after that, another, also devoid of life. We all began to dread seeing hills sticking up above the water, any signs that there may have been life. The mystery ate at our minds and into our dreams, making us stir from our sleep in the night.

If we'd found a fourth village without any people in it, I might have called the whole operation off, scared of what might have caused such a depopulation, but to our luck we didn't find such a thing. No, in what had to have been the largest spot of dry land yet, we found a sprawling cadre of homes and visible figures walking about. We even saw a boat or two out on the water, spears in hands showing they were fishing.

People waved, perking up and calling out as we approached, a few pointing us to their own little landing area. However I noticed that it, too, seemed to hold fewer boats than I'd expected, even if some were out working for the day.

"Welcome, strangers," one of the locals said as he came to meet us. "You're lucky to have caught us before we finished packing our things. Heading inland?"

"Yes, from far off, though. Where is everyone?" I inquired. "We've seen nothing but abandoned villages for weeks."

If there was one thing I loved about elven society, it was that linguistic drift was nearly zero. With crotchety ancients demanding others speak as they did, and the fact that we could live theoretically forever, everywhere we went speech was intelligible. One only need to look briefly at British linguistic history to know that wasn't normal on Earth.

"Oh, I see. Well come sit with me, and I'll tell you what you need to know."

CHAPTER 40

ANSWERS

"I suppose you don't know the details, so let me start at the beginning," our host, an elf named Curz, began. He sat down and gestured for us to do the same. "About a hundred years ago, we suffered a rather large monster incursion. The main holdings of the local ancient, Tia, were beset by a flying beast of impressive proportions. I wasn't there, but I was told it was a bird of some form, coming from the east, and that it ripped and tore apart everything it found."

"So there were a lot of deaths?" I asked.

"Oh, hundreds and hundreds, yes. Villages uprooted, warriors slaughtered. Old Tia, our leader, gathered a band of her strongest and led a charge against the beast. It was through great sacrifice that they slew it, though, in turn it took the life of Tia. She struck it down at the cost of her own life, and the lives of many of her most powerful followers—children and old elders, who battered the creature with her, half of them gone in a day." He looked sad as he spoke, and I supposed that made sense. He might even have known some who died.

"But they won though, right? So the deaths ended," Chien surmised.

"No, the killing had only just begun," he told us.

"Huh?"

"Nature abhors a vacuum," I explained. "That many of the strongest gone at once? Did the attacks come from inside or out?"

"In, slowly at first, but building. None of the survivors could match Tia's power, but three tried, one on each of the great hills. Lon the Mighty was the strongest, a warrior of power and speed. He took the largest hill in the middle, and to his sides were Uro the Singer and Nora the Healer. Lon gathered the absolute strongest of the people to his cause, though there were few. Uro was the second strongest, attracting most of the elders, whom he had better connections with, but the weaker folk loved Nora and flocked to her banner like fish to bait."

"And the state of things now?" Isha asked.

"Lon fell ten years ago to a combined attack. His forces too few and each loss too deep a wound. Since then, there's been several attempts at peace, but neither leader wants to bend to the other. Nora's forces grow but are still weaker on average, whereas Uro now suffers much like Lon did. Both are entrenched deeply and are constantly trying to gather more supporters."

"I'm guessing most of the villages moved to support one or the other? Promises of high rewards to tempt the strong while the weak were fearful of staying behind unguarded?" I surmised.

"You've seen such a thing before?" he asked.

"Not personally, but it makes sense. Out of curiosity, who does your village support? Bearing in mind that we're outsiders with no care for who wins or loses."

He chuckled. "Nora; she's promised us better lands with easier hunting and more room for homes. Most of the further out villages do, as the inner ones have long denied us good lands."

I sighed. "We're messengers, here to talk to the leader. We'll have to talk to both."

"Unlikely, friend," he replied. "They're at war. Think they'll just let you walk across the border? You have to make a choice."

"Says who?"

"Says the world."

For a moment I looked at him, readying to strike if needed. "If I try to choose Uro, what will you do?"

"Nothing, though I'd want you to change your mind." He sat back, calm as could be.

"Why?"

"Two reasons," he said, leaning in, as if conspiring. "One, your boat is nice and big, and if you want to talk to Nora, I could arrange it, should you help us move inward. And two, it'll be safer. Think about it, traveler. You've come all this way; you must surely know how to fight. Maybe even learned some things in the war you were in, huh? You said one ancient killed another, so you know the old ones can die, and have seen it done."

"I'm uninterested in settling here," I told him, looking back at my companions.

"Perhaps so, perhaps so, but I think if you talk to our lady, she'll convince you, and if I know her, she won't object if you leave afterward."

"We'll need to think about it."

I gathered my companions and we returned to our boat. Nobody seemed to want to stop us, apparently convinced that we'd be convinced. Honestly, though, I had my doubts.

"What do you two think?" I asked them when we'd retreated.

"There's got to be a way to let them both know," Chien said.

"Does it even matter? We can tell this Nora, and if she loses the contest for succession, we tried," Isha said with a shrug.

"Maybe, but I don't want to be involved in this conflict."

"You, avoiding conflict? That might be a first," she quipped, but backed off when I glared.

"I don't like it, even if I am good at it."

"Eh," my assistant said. "Better to not like fighting and be good at it than like fighting and be bad at it."

"That's refreshingly deep, Chien. However, we still don't have an answer."

"Take out both of them and rule instead?" Chien jokingly suggested.

"Why would I want to?" I asked.

"How should I know? I'm just saying you could, probably."

That was entirely unhelpful. Though, I had to consider for a moment he might be right. With enough preparation time and some hard work, I might be able to do something similar to what I'd done to Cino during the war in Atal, but why? I didn't really want to rule these lands, and I certainly didn't like killing. Nor did I care to draw attention to the fact that I could potentially create multiple ancient-killing weapons.

"Screw it," I said. "We go with Isha's suggestion. We'll let this Nora know what happened, and if we get a chance to send word across the lines, we do it, but there's no proper ruler here. I'd like to do a better job of it, but unless one of them wins by the time we get there, nobody's truly in charge."

They both agreed with a shrug. After all, it really was the best we could do.

CHAPTER 41

PACKING UP

Our hosts were delighted that we were coming with them. I suspected that it was because we had a big honking boat, several times larger than one of their canoes. They did indeed ask that we carry some of their stuff, and people too, but I nixed the latter part of the request. I didn't know these people, so I didn't want them to do anything unpleasant on my vessel.

Of course, I was getting something for hauling their stuff; several things, in fact. First, I was getting their knowledge of the region. They knew the swamps and the paths toward the center far better than I. I was also getting them as guards. Some beasts would attack our small group as we traveled, but a larger group like we were now forming would give pause to even the largest of monsters in this world.

There was no elder in this village, he and all of his closest people having left some time ago. Instead, I ended up negotiating with Curz.

"So, why'd you stay?" I asked as we tied down the goods in our craft. "After the elder left, you mean?"

"Yes."

"Thought I could take over, reestablish. Seemed a better idea than going and getting involved in the war. I'm nearly old enough to have my own village, but my power just started making itself known, so it'd be some time yet before I could establish one personally."

That wasn't too odd. While all elves had the potential for magic, and even the weakest had some small trick, true ability was rarer among us. I'd even heard that as we aged, the chances that it would blossom into something more increased, with every elder I'd ever heard of having some magical talent.

"So, what happened?" Chien asked, pulling the rope-like vine that we were using taut and flashing a quick knot into it.

"Too weak, honestly. I'd like to say it's not a problem, but we've had a few close calls, and I wasn't as strong as I'd needed to be to deal with them easily. Most of our best hunters and the like left too; without them the village is indefensible in the long run."

"You're giving up on it then?" my assistant asked.

"No, not forever. What I'm doing is taking the time I need to prepare properly. Surely a traveler understands that?"

"We do," I assured him. "And I suspect that's what's been happening all over the place. A few of the strongest leave, then there's just not enough for all that needs done."

"Hmm, at any rate, we are thankful for your aid. Would've had to make some hard decisions on how to do things or make new boats, but with yours we can leave soon." Even if we weren't taking passengers, having extra room since they no longer needed to worry about the stuff helped.

"And we yours. It would take forever to find where we're going without a proper guide."

"On the subject of boats, don't suppose you'll tell me how you made yours? I've never seen the like."

"It's not a secret," I said with a shrug. "While we're going I can teach you how. As with most things there are ups and downs to any way of doing things."

He nodded at that and left us.

"He's touchy," Chien said as the man left to go deal with the others leaving, which was everyone left in the village.

"He's leaving his home and not in good straits. Even if Curz isn't showing it, he's under a lot of pressure."

"Why?"

"Would you be so relaxed if you were leaving not only your home but your family?" I asked.

"You've seen me leave both my home and family."

I pulled up short at that; he was right. Chien hadn't needed to come with us on this journey, but he had. He'd also left everything behind—all the people he knew, all the places—and he'd come without so much as blinking. That felt sort of sad to me, but I wasn't sure I could really stand in judgment. After all, I'd left my home multiple times now.

"Fair point," I said after a time. "But most people are a lot more attached to those things than you seem to be."

"Nah, I've just got my priorities straight. Cities and towns are just buildings, and as for my family, we don't really get along. It's an important thing, Justin, to know what you need to care about and what you don't." Now he was giving me advice.

I just shook my head. "I always forget what you're like, still seeing you as that kid I met all those years ago."

"Haven't changed much honestly, though I'm a lot stronger now."

"That you are, and hornier too."

"Nothing wrong with that," he said, puffing out his chest.

"I'm proud of you, Chien. You worked hard to get where you are."

He looked at me with a smile, the joking gone for just a second. "Thanks, boss."

We had just enough room left in the boat for our own things and to sleep, if of course we slept atop some of the gear. Honestly, as I looked over the gear that these villagers were having us transport, I almost scoffed, but then I remembered myself. Their tools looked much like the ones my own village had so long ago, before I'd begun introducing metal and ceramics, before I'd taught them some of the simpler methods I knew. No, as I looked at the tools and goods piled up, I realized that for this world these weren't trash but prized possessions. It was me who was odd.

Perhaps I should work more on spreading those techniques; maybe not all of them, but some of them. This world would grow, would change, would improve. Then I realized that now really wasn't the time for these people. They were in the middle of a war, and my intervention would only spur one side or the other to be far more interested in me than I wanted. I'd teach them the boat technique, as I'd promised, then nothing else. That would do fine.

CHAPTER 42

FLOTILLA

While we were slowed by our guides, they more than made up for it with their knowledge. Not just knowledge of the surroundings, though they had that in spades, but of the flora and fauna of the swamp. They knew how to keep the turtles from bothering us, to keep the gators at bay. We were shown the herbs that made foods taste better and where to find the best berries. Also, though we were not moving as fast, we were moving in a definite direction.

The highways and byways of the swamp were there, but they could easily be missed in the massive region that comprised this place. Currents meandered around zones of marsh that hardly moved, winding in and out and around. They didn't even stay completely stable, with changes in the environment moving the routes we'd need to take to get where we were going, but a well-minded hand could find them and follow them to their destination.

So, our days were spent thus, days turning to weeks, drifting toward the next stop on our journey. We learned but stayed distant, keeping well back from the villagers we knew we'd be leaving at some point. After all, we'd already made so many new acquaintances, and none of us were planning on staying. Curz, however, did come by from time to time.

About a month in, he joined us on a larger section of ground, one of the many former villages we were passing through. There'd been several, and more where people had opted to join our little caravan, throwing their lot in with the larger group headed deeper into the swamp.

"Justin," he said, sitting down. "You said you wouldn't mind showing me how to build boats like yours?"

"I don't, but why now?" I asked, having assumed he'd wait until we got to our destination at this point.

"One of our scouts came back from the next village ahead, and all of them want to join us. We don't have enough rafts for that, much less enough good ones. It would be some help if we could have more."

"Probably be faster to make normal rafts, but might be better to use ones like ours for any children . . ." Regardless of how much I might have started out different, there was no stopping the change toward the culture that was all around you, and I felt some need to protect kids quite a bit more nowadays.

"Mmm, so?" he continued.

"We'll need some time, a day or two, even if we rush it," I pointed out to him.

"Should be fine," he replied. "The village will take a few days at the least to pack their things and prepare what they can, and this is a better place to rest—more room and plenty of dry ground."

"Chien?" I called, looking over at my assistant. "Care to join us?"

"Sure thing, boss."

The three of us grabbed a couple of the other villagers for extra muscle and headed out into the swamp. Rubber trees, like the ones we'd used weren't uncommon, and while they might not be everywhere, they were certainly easy enough to find. Our companions were particularly helpful with this, as they were more familiar with the environment, leading us to excellent specimens.

We harvested a glut of the rubber bark, sheets and sheets, pulling it back to the camp en masse and lashing the wood into makeshift rafts. We needed more of those anyway, so why waste the wood? With the help we had, we gathered easily enough for three vessels just like ours in only a few hours, many hands making light work. I noted that I needed to do more things like this; groups were able to make stuff happen so much faster.

The men and women of the swamp gawked at us as we unloaded our haul and didn't stop as we began the construction process. Chien and I led, but I was once again reminded that the locals of this world weren't stupid. They just lacked the knowledge of my old world. Their paradigm hadn't shifted toward where mine was, not seeing some of the use in materials that I'd taken for granted.

"I see a problem," Curz said as we worked on the first, magic making the needle that would bind it together flit in and out at high speed.

"What's that?" I asked.

"We don't have those," he said, pointing to the little iron tool.

"Ah, that's true, but you don't need to have one like that. One made of bone should work, though you may need to use the bones of a strong creature to make it if you want it durable enough." I wasn't sure, honestly, having done fairly little work with bone needles, but I knew that they weren't normally as durable or sharp.

"Is that what you did then, use the bones of a powerful beast? I'll admit I've never seen a material like that before."

"No, this is made from a certain rock from my homeland." While true, it wasn't particularly descriptive. "It would be hard to acquire here, but if you want to trade for one, I have a few pieces I could make."

He seemed to waffle for a moment before nodding. I could make him a new needle later. The process was simple, and I'd win goodwill for it. Both of us would get what we wanted, and while I knew that bog iron was a thing, I also knew that it wasn't exactly easy to gather, nor where I might find it in this massive morass of a wetland.

It took a lot of work, but after three days we'd produced three boats—all that we could with the bark we'd brought in. Word came that the village should be ready for us to leave now, and so a newly grown flotilla of rafts plodded down toward the next village over.

When we arrived, the people were gathered on the shore, bustling and rushing to and fro. Bundles of goods, food, tools, and personal effects were piled high on their own boats or up along the shore. Children were being herded, with families trying to keep things together as they looked for anything missed. It looked like absolute chaos, and I was pleased that most of my part in this mess was done.

We did end up helping with the loading a bit, but only because we had little else to do. I'd never felt right sitting back and watching while others struggled with a task, so a little lifting and the like wasn't a chore at all.

As we were all about halfway done loading, a man from the village ran up to shore, eyes wide. He headed to Curz and someone whom I could only assume was the local leader, though she wasn't an elder either. It seemed the oldest of our kind had truly abandoned their homes. I heard the approaching elf, as did many others when he spoke, breathless and clearly alarmed.

"A group is approaching fast, ten strong, and all look to have some ability," the scout said in a panic.

CHAPTER 43

MASS ABDUCTION

The canoes that made their way up to the little village weren't the normal make. Most of the people here used rafts lashed together with vines and the like. Rafts were slow but had carrying capacity unrivaled by other craft, so they made excellent vessels for hunters who needed to carry back their kills or, in our case, for travelers who were carrying their stuff.

These boats, however, were much faster—sleek and cut through the water like knives. They weren't complex things, mostly just trees cut in half and shaped by stone ax, but it was like night and day. The small boats held little in the way of supplies, instead holding only armed men.

Our main problem, though, was that all of those approaching had the telltale glow of aura about them. That meant that each and every one of these men had magic of some form. It didn't mean they were all casters, but it meant that they were all dangerous. The only saving grace was that none displayed the shocks of white hair that designated them as an elder.

I stood well back as they landed. After all, this wasn't my village. Each of them looked interested in the buzz of activity that had stopped as they came near, younger, weaker elves backing away as the intruders joined them.

One of them who appeared to be a leader of some form stepped from his boat, a few of the others mimicking his actions. He walked over to one of the rubber craft I'd made for the locals and poked its side several times, eventually earning an echoing *phonk* from the boat.

"Interesting," the interloper said loudly enough for everyone around to hear him.

The nominal leader of this village slowly began to approach. She was a caster of some form, but not a particularly powerful one. Several of the newcomers' eyes flicked up in recognition, including their leader's. He then took the time to look around at the others nearby, clearly looking for auras. I saw recognition in his eyes when he spotted my little group. The three of us together made him raise his eyebrows.

"Greetings, traveler," the village leader said. She was a healer named Effa. "What brings you to our village today?"

"Ah, you must be the head of this village now? Or is your elder about?" he asked the woman.

"Unfortunately not," Effa replied. "Elder Lysa left some time ago to head toward the cities. As you can see we're planning to follow her shortly."

"Of course, of course, my apologies. Where are my manners? My name is Kar, and our benevolent leader, Uro, has heard of your evacuations. He knows that with the elders leaving as they are, your villages are now under threat, and in kind understanding has sent us to help you on the path to the cities." As he spoke I could see the men behind him smile, but they tightened their stances, clearly ready to fight.

I wanted to curse, to rage, but I held my peace. It was clear what was going on here. This was a mass kidnapping. Uro knew that people were going to his opposition in large numbers, so he sent people to bring them to him instead, meat for the grinder of his war machine. If the village resisted, or tried to insist they were going to Nora's side instead, it was obvious what would happen.

There were ten of them, ten proper magic users armed and no doubt trained to fight, and given the situation probably more skilled than most. Could we beat them in a straight fight? Doubtful, but even if we could, there would be losses. Curz and Effa were the only two full magic users from the collective villages. Others were either too weak to be useful or too young to fight. If we fought, we'd likely lose, and should we win but lose the casters, the rest of the group would be left without any protection from real threats.

Chien moved to stand alongside me, and Isha moved behind me. The three of us had seen war before, and both Chien and I had killed our own kind when we defended Atal.

"Boss?" my assistant asked.

"Watch and wait," I said.

Effa and Kar had stared each other down, the woman seeming to weigh her options. It dragged on for seconds before she finally spoke.

"I see," she said noncommittally. "May I have a moment to speak with the leader of one of the other villages joining us? To plan things out."

"Certainly," the kidnapper said with a smile. "Take all the time you need. After all, we're in no rush."

Effa rushed off to Curz, pulling him away and toward one of the nearby huts. Seeing this, Kar slowly walked over to our group, eyebrow quirked.

"Greetings, friend," he said neutrally, seeming to come to some conclusion. "I can't help but notice they didn't consult you? Nor can I help but notice your clothes are different from the people here. Are you perhaps from some village further out?"

"Messengers," I responded calmly. I didn't like the man, but starting a fight wasn't to my advantage right now. "From far off to report the deaths of Atal and Cino to the local leaders."

Kar looked at me confused, but behind him I heard a hiss from one of his companions.

"I . . . don't know who that is?" he said, looking back toward the other warriors.

"Ancients, both from the north, Kar. Uro will want to know. This is terrible news," the other one confirmed, looking solemn.

It was terrible news. Three ancients down in such a short amount of time was unheard of. Two was a tragedy, leaving a whole section of our continent without leadership. As it stood, everything in the south was now devoid of the protection that an ancient alone could provide. There was nobody to call for help if another large monster showed up, nobody who might be able to send meaningful aid.

Massive monsters like the one who'd killed the previous leader of the swamps were rare, but not unheard of in this world, and they were counted as something like a natural disaster of incredible proportions. It was like Krakatoa or the Tunguska event. Things happened, but they were rare.

Kar looked at us. "Messengers, you are welcome to join us, to tell Uro of your story. As we're headed in that direction already, I hope you have no objections?"

I did, and I was already considering ways to deal with him and his men, but that would depend on other things. How did he treat the villagers he was strong-arming onto their side? How did he respond to us? It would matter, but what didn't matter was that telling either Uro or Nora was already my goal. If these men became a problem . . . well I'd killed plenty of our kind before, and I even had a few of the small heating crystals stashed away if I needed them for explosions.

With a nod, I assured him it would be fine. Effa and Curz joined us shortly, the latter shooting me looks. They'd spoken briefly, probably to weigh their options, and decided that going with these warriors would be acceptable. It wasn't lost on me, though, that they'd made that decision because they didn't have a choice.

CHAPTER 44

MEMORIES OF HOME

About those boats," Kar said as the villagers went back to their preparations, stopping only to shoot periodic glances at Curz and his group, as well as mine.

"What about them?" I asked, holding back a sigh. I could already see the villagers turning inward and against us.

"You provided them, no? I don't think I've seen the like before, and it would make sense if someone from far away brought different things."

He wasn't wrong, but I was divided. On the one hand, I really didn't like these guys. They were going around strong-arming people into joining their team. That was understandable on some level, as there was a war on, and they at least hadn't been violent, yet, but it grated against my experiences from my previous world. Having been raised where freedom was one of the core values, seeing behavior like this was quite unwelcome.

On the other hand, spreading information like this would help the world and our people as a whole. This type of boat wasn't immediately weaponizable, nor was it too complicated. It would require some work for them to make themselves, but nothing they couldn't manage already, and the materials were locally sourced.

There was also the consideration of the war. Any information that provided even things that would help the people in general might serve to push the scales up or down on either side. The villagers would know, and while I doubted they'd do anything, being around unhappy people wasn't enjoyable. It might also get back to Nora that I was providing them with technology, even if I'd already given it to Curz, and I might have an unhappy elder to deal with.

"I did, but if we're to leave soon, I don't have the time to show you how," I said after carefully weighing my options. In the end, I decided that denying him wouldn't work and that pissing off either side was a poor idea.

"Very interesting," he said. "You know, even if you are a messenger, you could stay. We always have need for people with sharp minds and power in their blood, and Uro is no fool. I imagine he'd treat you well."

"Thank you for letting me know," I said noncommittally, having received similar offers a number of times already and denied them all.

I expected the villagers to drag their feet but was surprised when they were ready to go in only a few hours. Perhaps they understood that dragging things out wouldn't help them, or that it would only irritate the men who were here to "escort" them along. Perhaps they had some sort of plan; I didn't honestly know.

That evening we ended up camping on another small island. It wasn't too far from where we'd begun, but with the number of people we had and the speed we were traveling—something around the speed of a mighty starfish—it was clear to me that this was going to be a long trip.

Kar and his men camped farther away from us, with pairs of them breaking into groups for watch schedules. Chien, Isha, and I set up our own watches, of course, as did the villagers. None of the groups truly trusting one another. As we prepared our dinner, Curz came to join us.

"Hello, Curz."

The sound around us muted—some spell of his, if I had to guess.

"Did you lead them to us?" he asked accusingly.

"No."

"Did you know they were coming?"

"I did not."

"But you're fine with going with them? After this nonsense?" He was angry, and it was clear to see that he was trying to judge where our group would fall.

"Uro is as likely as your patron to let me leave and will fulfill my mission to spread the news just as effectively. This is not my fight, Curz, and while I may not like these men, there's a difference between that and wanting to go to war."

"Pfft, what would a coward like you know of war?" he spat, causing both Isha and Chien to look up.

"How many of our kind have you killed, Curz?" I asked.

"That's not—" he tried before I cut him off.

I stood, drawing close to him, eyes unblinking. "Because I have killed many. The first I killed when I was still a boy, a threat to my people and my home that couldn't be removed any other way. Then, when war came to Atal, I killed more, units of soldiers. In the final battle between our forces, I rained fire and death upon our enemies."

"You . . ." he tried, clearly shaken by my displeasure as I let loose my magic, feeling it flow out and seeing the bubbling aura that surrounded me expand like a cloud.

"*I* know what comes of war, because I've seen what it brings. Friends and foes broken and ripped apart, gasping for air that won't come, screaming as they die. There is a time to fight, and a time not to, and right now there are too many innocents in the way."

"So . . . so you'll help us? If we can get the others to safety."

"You weren't listening. This isn't my fight. All I want is to do my job and go home." He deflated, looking around in worry. "Though I won't stop you should you do something. That is on you."

For a moment the leader thought, eyes low as he considered things.

"If I should, and if I should fail, will you see that the villagers make it to safety?"

"I've nothing against your people, and I need them to guide me. If things go awry, I will do what I can to keep them safe, at least until we reach the cities."

He nodded and left us, looking like a man ready to die.I went to sit down in our raft, unhappy with everything going on. Isha and Chien had been present for the conversation, but Chien had said nothing, probably because he didn't actually care. Isha joined me where I sat, rubbing my back gently.

"Are you okay?" she asked.

"I'm tired, love. I'm tired, and I want to go home." I looked at her as I spoke. "You haven't told me anything about what you think of this."

For a moment she looked off into the distance, pursing her lips and thinking.

"I really don't know, Justin, I really don't. I've never been in a situation quite like this, so I'll trust your judgment on the matter." Her piece said, she kissed my cheek.

"You're not worried that I'm making the wrong choice?"

"No." She simply shrugged. "You may be a mess, but you tend to do better than I would in wild situations."

"Whatever comes, I'll keep you safe."

"I love you too."

CHAPTER 45

TERMS

Curz and his people were strangely silent for the next few days. Sure, there were one or two small incidents where people stepped on each other's toes, but no attacks, no fighting beyond words. In the background, though, there was looking, watching, waiting. It was impossible not to notice them, not to see that they were planning . . . something.

"Mind if I have a word?" Kar asked a few days in, hopping over to my boat with a bit of magic I couldn't quite catch.

"I do not," I answered tiredly.

"I have a question," he stated.

"Please ask."

"I believe that the villagers are planning something. However, I can't help but notice that you're not joining in. From one outsider to another, and so you're not caught unprepared, I wanted to let you know that there could be some danger for you and yours."

I sighed. "If they have an issue, it would be with you, not me, Kar. You and your men are the ones who are forcing them into your camp."

He feigned shock. "No, certainly these people are loyal to Uro. Even you should be able to see that." I just stared at him for a few moments before he laughed. "All right, I suppose there's no need for deceit, not between us."

"Since there's no need for deception, what can I help you with?" I asked as Isha watched on from behind and Chien snoozed.

"If and when things fall apart, I wanted to know whose side you'd be on."

"Mine," I answered.

"Not a horrible answer, but hardly the clarity I was hoping for," the other elf said, narrowing his eyes.

"I will not attack you and your men, nor will I help you if should be attacked by others. How is that?"

"So you're staying out of it?"

"Yes."

"I don't suppose you've told this to the villagers, have you?"

"If I had and told you, that would confirm your suspicions, wouldn't it? But, if they asked me, that is also what I would tell them."

"Good to know. Do you mind if I ask you for a small favor? Well, two, actually."

"And what are those?" I said, slowing the boat. We were pulling away more than I'd like, and I didn't want to be too far from the others.

"If something happens, will you protect the villagers, particularly the children? They're a precious thing, and I'd hate to see them harmed. Not those attacking us, mind you, but those who would stay out of the way." I managed not to laugh. His opposite had asked me nearly the exact same thing.

"Certainly, and what's the other."

"Try to convince them not to do something."

"Kar, while I appreciate what you're asking, I think you've over-estimated what exactly I can do here. As you said earlier, I'm an outsider too."

"True, but one who isn't hated like I am, one who's neutral, one who might keep me and my men from having to slaughter people whom we'd much rather just come along peacefully. I might even lose some of my people or myself if they decide to attack, and I don't much like that. What I want is for these villagers to come along quietly. Partially because I believe it will be better for them in the end anyway."

"Why do you believe that?" I asked honestly.

"Because I know Uro, and I knew Nora, and I know which will make a better leader. Don't get me wrong, Nora's not a bad person, but she's not suited to rule. For now it seems fine, but in time I fear that she'll become a tyrant, and a horrible one at that." That made me blink. "Also, we plan to win, and having more people safely on our side helps."

"I hate to say it, Kar, but from everything I've heard, Nora seems . . . Well, people think she's pretty nice."

"Do you know why nearly all of the older people are now with Uro?" he asked.

"Because he promised you power and land?" I guessed.

"Yes, but no. We know her; we've known her for a long time. The swamps aren't so big that all of the elders here haven't met. She is nice, at least most of the time, but she's also capricious, and has a cruel streak when she wants to."

That gave me a lot of things to think about. In my lives I'd known a lot of things, and one of those was that women who were cruel could be really, really cruel, and they could hide it alarmingly well. But you couldn't hide anything forever, and we lived a long, long time. However, I couldn't take this man purely at his word either, as he was, of course, from an opposing force.

"I'll talk to them, and tell them that you don't want to fight," I said. "Can't promise that will change anyone's mind, but it will let them know that. Honestly though, you should be the one talking to them."

"Wouldn't listen to me, Justin, but might listen to you."

"Very well."

That night when we made camp I went to join Curz during dinner, if only for a moment. The man looked up surprised and initially very welcoming, until I sat down and began to speak.

"That's the basic message," I said. "They know you want to fight, but they don't want to," I said after a short explanation.

"And they sent you to tell us?" he almost accused, face flashing between confusion and anger.

"Thought you might listen to me better. I'll say this, though—he did at least ask me to look after the villagers if something happened. Means that while I may disagree with what he's doing, he isn't a maniac."

"Pah, that's not worth anything." The leader looked displeased, none present looking any better. "Could also be that he was seeing who you'd go to tell, getting you to lead him to those in charge."

"Which is why I went to three fires before this one, and will go to several afterward. I'm not a fool, Curz, and I'd appreciate it if you didn't treat me like one."

"My apologies, but it changes nothing."

"That is your decision, not mine," I finally answered. If they were determined to fight and die, well, there was little I could do about it.

Another week passed, and if what I was hearing was correct, we were finally nearing the outer territories of both cities. We were closer to Uro's actual region, but the two had to be near one another because of how the borders worked and the pathways flowed.

We turned off into a small pool to wait for the slower rafts to catch up when it happened. Several people from the villages surged forth, spells flying from their hands.

"Shit," Chien said groggily from behind me, having been taking more of the night shifts.

"Yeah," I replied, spinning shields into existence around us.

CHAPTER 46

MARSHLAND BATTLE

Over a dozen different attacks of various kinds headed toward the empowered soldiers. I saw no less than three spears hurled at speeds that would surely destroy them, in addition to two bolts of fire, three of water, and one, surprisingly, that looked like electricity and left a small afterimage in my vision. There were also two bolts of esoteric energies that screamed danger and an attack I couldn't quite identify. These were mixed in with some more normal spears and stones that were being hurled, but not at nearly the same danger level.

Kar and his men were quick to respond, though not quite quick enough. I saw counter attacks fly forth, exploding in midair to disrupt what they could, and weapons flash outward to clash against other projectiles. Oddly, I didn't see any shield bubbles like I used. Either they avoided them for some reason or didn't think to do something like that.

Chien pulled the boat back with his magic as I continued to pump protections around us. This was all according to plan, as both of us knew my magic was still quite a bit stronger than his. For her part, Isha was already starting to sing, and I felt a light pulse of power from her. She didn't use her magic as much as either of us for combat, but it felt like she was trying to begin healing, even if there was no need just yet.

Three of the soldiers looked injured, struck here and there, but not yet completely out of the fight. The others, though, looked quite serious, angry at the pain inflicted upon their fellows, determined to stop the assault.

"They're going to be crushed," Chien observed as we settled near the boats full of bystanders.

"Look, there's something missing," I pointed out as I wove a much larger shield around the innocents, pushing it outward to slow or deflect any stray attacks.

"Curz and the other caster," Isha whispered.

Kar and his men didn't notice several of their outriders launching themselves at the attackers. The physically enhanced individuals were strong and alarmingly fast, and trying to push through the formation of about twenty who were assaulting them.

Some of the villagers leapt forward at the oncoming soldiers. They looked to be hunters, and not senior ones. My guess was that most of the older ones had either left or were with Curz, wherever he'd run off to. The villagers weren't helpless, though. Upon them, small lines brightened, causing their skin to shine as the soldiers impacted. It was a telltale glow of magical tattoos, ones I'd not noticed on them until now, but the effect was obvious. The defenders became bulwarks, stopping dead the first round of strikes against them.

Even if I hadn't seen it before, it made sense. Hunters in these lands would need to contend with powerful animals, magical or otherwise, and having some type of defense would be a lifesaver. Did the soldiers know about those tattoos, though? Or expect them? After all, the images themselves had been well hidden enough that I'd not noticed them on the young elves' bodies.

It was at this moment that Curz decided to make himself known. From behind me, a series of powerful bolts blew forward, past my shielding, which had only been made to keep things out, and into the soldiers' boat. One went straight for Kar, but at the last moment he ducked, the attack striking the fighter beside him and blowing his head clean off. The pumping spray of blood into the air soaked those who'd held back on their own vessel. The other caster's series of attacks was no less effective, even if it was less thunderous, and killed two of the injured soldiers.

Kar and his people did the same thing I did—turned to see where the attacks had come from. Curz and I were definitely going to have a problem after this. I needed to know now where he'd hidden. He'd asked me to defend the innocents, and now he was among them, using them as living shields. I found them on one of the boats, slinging spells and standing among several other villagers who were preparing spears, right in the middle of the civilians' crafts.

I was still trying to figure out how to push my shield so it didn't cover them when the first impacts struck. It had only been designed to deflect, but the casters on Kar's side must have been using very different techniques than I was used to because their balls of flame and energy exploded when they impacted the barrier. Some of the spells were only deflected, but they flew so wide as to be useless.

The more muscle-inclined soldiers seemed to identify the true threat around this point and pivoted, with a couple taking attacks to the back when they did, all but one of them rounding on Curz's boat. The one that didn't turn toward him turned at us and sped forward across the water with murder in his eyes.

All three of our formations formed a sort of L-shape, with Kar's men being the meeting place of the two lines, the initial attack at the end of the short bottom line, and Curz and his personal forces at the top. I, of course, was situated right between Kar and Curz, directly in the line of fire from both sides.

Chien caught the oncoming physical soldier as he bounced against the much more thorough protections I'd woven around our craft. His spell was kinetic in nature and pretty impressive, similar to what had proven the end of Atal.

"Not your enemy, idiot!" Chien yelled before tossing the man in a high arc.

Curz, not letting a good moment pass, threw an attack, rendering the much slower soldier above him a burst of red chunky rain. That was four, four people he'd managed to kill because I was in the way, and it was enough for me. I pulled back my outer shield, dropping all protections on any who weren't my own.

This marked a turning point. While Curz and the other caster put up a good fight, without a physical magic user to defend them, their protectors quickly fell to the leftover soldiers. The initial attackers died screaming when Kar himself sent a fireball into their craft, leaving nothing but flaming splinters.

By the end, Uro's soldiers had lost six of their number, but they'd killed almost all of the attackers, leaving only Curz and a few of those on his boat still alive. The other village leader floated face up in the water, neck snapped so powerfully that it looked like she'd been born with a head facing the wrong direction.

None of those who hadn't attacked had been harmed, and that was a small blessing. Even if the two leaders of these villages had been determined to fight, some of their people were very young, or had simply hidden, paddling to the side of the river when things started to go down.

Kar called them all out now as he strode over to the leader across their tied together boats.

"Uro sent us to offer you his mercy. All you needed to do was not fight. We didn't want this, didn't want to harm you, didn't want to kill you. No, you brought this down upon your own head," Kar intoned, amplifying his voice enough that everyone could hear it.

"Liar, slaver, killer!" Curz spat at him, screaming as loudly as he could.

"Enough! See now what happens to those who refuse to accept mercy or kindness." Kar's men held Curz by the arms as he raised his hand, flames pouring out around it brighter and brighter.

It was clear he planned to burn the captured man to little more than bones, but before he could, a small, nearly invisible pinprick of light hit him in the chest. The spell took effect instantly, and he fell dead, his fire dissipating in a poof of air and smoke. Next were the two soldiers holding Curz, who died similarly before anyone could find the attacker.

"I heard there were disturbances and came to see for myself. This is not what I expected to find," a gentle feminine voice said. She was standing in the grasses to one side of the marsh.

Reeds parted and a number of elves, all clearly elders, strode out. At their head could be none other than Nora, with pure white hair that fell just to her shoulders. The last of Kar's soldiers tried to flee but hardly made it a step before they were torn apart by magic.

A bridge of vines grew where Nora walked, leading her to where the defeated leader lay sprawled on the ground. She leaned over Curz, smiling.

"Are you okay, dear? Don't worry, I'm here now."

CHAPTER 47

EXHAUSTING ELDERS

After Nora's arrival and the remnants of the fallen had been wiped clean, she saw to all of the villagers, if not personally, then one of her aides who had similar magic to herself. There was a clear delineation now between us and them, and some of them looked none too pleased.

I could understand their point. I'd done nothing to intentionally aid them, instead leaving the fighters out to dry. Then again, I'd also done exactly as I'd said I would do. I'd tried to help protect the innocent while letting those who wanted to fight, fight. So, I didn't really care to hear any of their complaints at the moment. I just wanted to talk to Nora and be done with this farce.

However, her people had opinions too. They could clearly see that me and mine had magic, and they could tell from what they saw that we'd done nothing to aid Curz in the fight or his impending execution, even though we could have. Several of her people kept an eye on us as she and the other healers saw to the injured, their gazes just short of hostile. But, I didn't run and didn't try to fight them, so they seemed content for the moment to wait, their defensive postures making sure we didn't try anything.

One of her people eventually brought a small raft over to our larger boat.

"Greetings," he began with a harsh tone.

"Greetings," I replied, keeping my own voice calm.

"The villagers are none too pleased with you. They say you didn't help them against the men trying to take them by force."

"I did not. I also told them I would not, and explained why in detail."

He snorted. "So I heard, but still, you can't think that was right?"

"The men you killed thought their leader was right, you think your leader is right. Who is right? I don't know. I'm not from here, nor do I plan to stay here. It is not my place to tell your people how to live if I don't plan to do anything for them," I answered with a shrug.

"You're defending that scum?!"

"No, I'm staying out of it. Did I defend them from you?" I asked, trying to get him to reason. "What about Curz and his attack? Did I defend them then?"

"That's . . . not untrue," he finally said.

"I've one thing I desire—to deliver my message and return home. Kindly ask your leader if she'd be willing . . ."

"No."

"No?"

"No, you're clearly not an ally. If you wish to speak with her, you will go through the proper channels."

I was taken aback by that. This world had its respect, its proper forms of address, and methods of seeking audience, but it was also far less formal than I was used to about that kind of thing. I was here. I needed to talk to her. She was here. The normal thing to do would be for one of her people to escort me over to her to do exactly that.

There was nothing stopping me from yelling my message or using magic to shout it across this damnable swamp. However, if I did so, her people would probably take rather great offense to it, and perhaps she would too. That would be bad, bad for me, bad for my companions, bad for this foolish, overly long mission.

"Very well," I said trying not to grit my teeth. "And how would I set up such a meeting to deliver my missive?"

"One of the counselors," he said. "There is always one on duty at her residence. I'm sure they would be perfectly happy to set up such a meeting." He managed to keep his face stony, but deep in his eyes I could see the smugness.

I considered violence in that moment. Violence was easy, and it was also effective, and I was good at it. I'd developed the weapons already, the methods for killing even those far stronger than myself. It wasn't always easy, but it was very doable. After all, we might be biologically ageless, but that didn't mean we didn't break and die.

"Very well, I shall do just that." As I spoke I felt the ice creep into my voice. He left then. He'd been an elder. That much was clear from the shock of white hair. What did that matter to me, though? Nothing. I was tired, tired of the power plays, tired of this swamp, tired of having to deal with curmudgeonly old elves. Still, just a bit further and we'd be done. I could live with them just a bit further.

"You good, boss?" Chien asked after a time. It was clear he sensed just how angry I was.

"Do we have any more of those heating crystals?" I asked quietly.

"A couple," Isha answered for him. "I kept them in case we needed them for trade, but I doubt you'll get anything for them here. Too warm."

"I would like them, please." I was glad we hadn't traded all of them, just in case an example needed to be made, or an escape if they decided we didn't need to leave their city.

"Okay . . ." She didn't argue, but instead began looking through our various bags.

While Isha was busy, Chien sidled up to me. "Boss, please don't do anything too extreme."

That brought me back to myself, the reminder that I didn't need much. I needed that from time to time—friends nearby to remind me who I was and what I should do. Sure, I was pissed off and tired, but killing senselessly? Raging and bringing pain to others without a good reason? No, that wasn't what I needed. I needed to be prepared if things went south, sure, but we weren't there. Not yet.

"Sorry if I lost myself a bit there, Chien. I'm just very tired of all this. Don't worry, I'll avoid any conflict with these folks, even if they do piss me off something fierce."

He patted me on the back cheerily. "That I understand, and you're a good person, boss. I'm sure everything will work out fine."

I sighed. "I'm not sure about being good, Chien, but I'm trying, and that's got to be worth something." He raised an eyebrow at that. "I've got my flaws, as you have yours. We fail, again and again, we fail. I've failed, more than once, and I'll fail again. I'm sure of that, but I'll try, try to do what's right."

"I know you will, boss."

CHAPTER 48

ARRIVING AT NORA'S

Water lapped at the side of our boat as we trudged along. Nora's people had made it clear, abundantly so, that we were not to approach her while traveling for safety reasons, or so they claimed. For that reason, and that reason alone, I was grinding my teeth as we moved through the early morning mist.

The swamps were, on the whole, kind of misty, but today we had bona fide pea soup in every direction. I could make out the other members of our little caravan, but anything far away? No, nothing in the distance was clear in the least. That was a shame because today we were supposed to be approaching our destination, hopefully the last one on this route before we could turn toward home.

As for our other companions, they were keeping their distance. The villagers weren't angry at us, per se, but they weren't totally happy either. That was understandable enough, as we had left them to their fates, but it didn't make the journey any more pleasant. Now there was a clear divide. Even the night before, it was obvious that they were setting up well away from us and we weren't welcome to come near them.

"So, when do you think we'll arrive?" Chien asked as the sun approached its zenith.

"Don't know, but not too much longer since we're supposed to get there today."

"Can't see anything with all this fog," Isha complained.

"Well, if we're being honest, do you want to see more swamp? I bet there's swamp around us, with swamp to one side, and swamp to the other. Oh, perhaps there's some marsh mixed in. What a refreshing change that would be. Can you even imagine?" Chien offered sarcastically.

"Oh yes, the tepid water, the smell of rotting vegetation. Whatever would we do without it?" I added.

She reached forward and pinched my ear like I was a naughty child.

"Ow!" I complained.

"Don't be a jerk then. There's supposed to be hills with settlements on them, and a lake. I'd love a proper lake after all this stupid . . ."

"Swamp?" Chien pointed out, only to get his own pinch.

It was shortly after that exchange that I realized the land around us was pulling back, opening up to a wider and wider lane. Soon the land that had surrounded our boats fell away completely, leaving us in open water.

The sun, in its great wisdom, got together with the wind and finally began doing their collective job. A warm gust passed, and bit by bit, the air began to clear.

We were in the lake, just off the shore to one side, and around us stood three massive hills. Each was equidistant from the others, dividing the central lake, which would probably take most of a day to sail around. It didn't look exactly like the rumors I'd heard, but it was also clear that this was a rather deep formation, with openings along the sides for boats to enter the central area.

"How in the world did this come to be?" Chien asked.

"Someone made it so," I said. "Look at how they're spaced, how the heights are the same. This isn't natural."

"An ancient?" Isha chimed in.

"I'd guess so, or a lot of work. Never underestimate the amount you can get done with just time and numbers."

"Look at that one, though," Isha said, nodding her head in one direction.

Two of the hills were clearly occupied, with obvious dwellings on them and even some visible people moving about here and there. The third, though, looked wrecked. Dirt or stone hadn't been removed, and the base was still fine, but it was clear to see that on the third hill the structures dotting it had been destroyed. Buildings were in ruins, crumbling and open. It was the second closest to us, but the smoke from fires was clearly far less than the other two hills.

"My guess is that was where our dead competitor was. As for who controls it now . . . who knows? Might even be where they're fighting. Shame, though. That would give them a whole other place to live, and with all these people coming in they're going to need it."

"Maybe they're bringing people in for when they need to fill out those places. With how few there are now, many must have died," Isha said. She was probably right.

I made my lens, expanding the view and focused on each of the hills as we moved slowly along. The two active ones had clear walls, patched, damaged, but maintained. People moved around inside them like ants whose hive had been disturbed, climbing and churning. There had to be thousands and thousands in this little place, even with all the war.

On the deserted hill there were still people, though fewer, and clearly ducking from street to street, hiding, just trying to survive with their homes. It looked like something from an old war movie, abounding with bombed-out homes and shattered places.

Architecture was another thing I noted. Everywhere I'd been was built a bit differently—here was no exception. Unlike the villages, which reminded me of home, these hills were hosting what looked to be mud-brick huts. That wasn't too surprising, given the supplies would dictate what they could use, but I wondered how they were insulating them against rain. The designs were simple, with mostly squares or circular shaped buildings. Each also supported a sizable dock, which no doubt meant that much of their food came from the lake in one way or another.

Each of the hills also sported what appeared to be a much larger residence atop it. Palaces for the rulers, no doubt. I could imagine that in times past, either the one who made this place moved from one to the other, or three ruled together. Perhaps I could find someone to ask about the history. With our long memories, someone certainly had to have heard something, even if they didn't see it themselves.

Soon enough, though, the front of our little column reached the docks, and a wave of cheering went up. It seemed the people here recognized their leader, and while I couldn't hear it fully, it was clear she was giving a speech. A small crowd had gathered, kept back by some of her guards, only for most of it to start moving up the hill behind her. Others stayed behind, helping the newcomers unpack their things and set up where they could.

In time, our turn came and we pulled into one of the little berths that someone on shore motioned us toward.

"Welcome, friend," the man said. "Do you have somewhere you're taking your things to?"

"No, not currently."

"Ah, I see," he replied. "Well, do you know anybody? Because I'll be honest, finding somewhere to stay isn't the easiest right now. All of the places the merchants were using are quite full up. You can always sleep in your boat if you want."

"Is there some charge for keeping it here?" I asked.

"Used to be, but Nora waved them all for now. With all you lot coming in from outside, there's nowhere for some folks to stay. Better they sleep somewhere safe than clog up the streets at night, right?" he said, laughing. "No worries, though. Once the war is over we'll be moving a lot of people to some of the homes from the other hills. Might have to do some repairs, but good, dry land isn't easy to come by."

"Of course, thank you. I hate to ask, but I really need to have a meeting with Nora. Her home is at the top, isn't it?"

"Where else would it be?" A fair point honestly.

"Just wanted to confirm, and thank you again," I told him before he left.

I asked Chien and Isha to wait at the boat, and then I began the climb upward.

CHAPTER 49

HURRY UP AND WAIT

The roads here were packed dirt, old and full to the brim. Walking through them was no challenge, though, as people had learned to move around like they would in any large city. Bare feet trod carefully across the winding paths, weaving between buildings like streams through a forest. Rather than going down like water, though, I was heading up, always upward to the top.

I'd forgotten so much about Atal, which came roaring back to me on this short walk. All around, people were shouting about their wares or goods, places to stay, services for this or that. Then there were the smells. Heavens, the smells. Atal always had a slightly fishy smell, being on the coast as it was, but here, in . . . Actually I didn't know the name of this city, not that it mattered, but it smelled of cooked food and elven waste.

One sound I realized I was missing was that of a smithy. I may have been running both the biggest and best one in our home city, but there were others. That was a respectable profession. The desire to build and improve was something I'd always get behind, and

I'd even shared some basic details with those back home; not too much, though. I was eager to see what they might come up with on their own.

Things got less crowded as I climbed higher. The homes were slightly bigger, if no further apart. The people had more decorations and complex clothing, but they were made from the local skins rather than the shells and beads that would have shown wealth in Atal. It was all a reminder of how things were so different.

Nora's home was easy to find. It had its own wall, smaller than some I'd seen, but impressive, with buildings and, I suspected, gardens behind it. At a few places along the top and at the gates were men in armor. That seemed odd. Her companions hadn't worn armor out in the field, but each of these men had breast-plates made of thick hide, hardened somehow. On one arm each soldier held a spear, tipped with some kind of bone, or spine protrusion, a slight sheen indicating possible poison, and on the other was a shield, crafted from turtle shell, but looking quite durable.

"Good afternoon," I began, approaching one of them cautiously.

"Hello . . ." he said, looking at me awkwardly. Apparently that wasn't a saying in these parts.

"I'm a messenger, here with one for Nora," I explained with a slight smile.

"Oh, I see," he replied. "One moment."

The soldier I was speaking to disappeared into the gate, and I was made to wait. Waiting seemed to be a thing I was doing entirely too much of with these people. Eventually, though, he appeared with a smallish woman following along. She was no elder, and no magic user; I could tell from a single look.

"Please come with me, esteemed messenger," she offered cheerily.

After getting my name and where I was from, I was left in a waiting room. Hour after hour I waited, tapping my fingers on the little stone table, until eventually my guide returned.

"Ah, my apologies," the woman said. "It seems her schedule was full today. Could you perhaps come back tomorrow?" she asked sweetly.

"Certainly," I answered with a forced smile.

Two more days passed without change. I came in the morning, was taken to the same room, and sat there until sundown neared. Sure, it seemed like a massive waste of time, and it was, but it didn't mean that nothing was getting done. Petty power plays were something I was used to, and I'd already developed a way to sort them out.

As I returned the evening of the third day of waiting, I looked at my companions. "So, what does this city want?"

"Places to stay," Isha answered. "They're desperate for housing, and food too, but that would be hard to improve, I think."

"Weapons," Chien said with a frown, knowing well how I felt about distributing those to anyone or everyone. "Boats too. I've had a number of inquiries about ours, but it looks like others are intercepting them with the information on that."

"Not surprising," I said. "We've shared that information already, so it's not like we can control it now."

"So what do we offer?" Isha asked.

"Something they need. Tomorrow we'll begin. Do we have the funds?" I asked.

"For what?" Chien inquired.

"All of the ashes in the city."

"We may . . ." Isha answered, still in charge of our finances. "What are you thinking?"

"Cement," I declared. "Best thing for fortifications they can get, and expands their space regardless. Not something they can turn down once they realize it. We'll also need the rights to a spit of the water."

I spent most of the rest of the evening making gems—nothing fancy, just a few of the different types that I'd learned to make over the years. These would serve as our currency, and we'd have to act fast, beating out the inflation that was sure to come.

As the sun crested the next morning, I changed up my schedule, seeking out other administrators while Chien and Isha went about getting the ingredients we needed for what was on the way. They were more than happy to part with a little spit of swampy ground for the bounty I offered them—a bounty that would be nigh worthless by sunset. I even managed to get a rental on a little open area where we could work in the city. Quite generous.

Chien arrived with materials all day, as did Isha, and both began helping me work. The former had worked with me on this before, so there was little need for speaking as he started to cast block after block of the liquid stone.

An hour or two before sundown I broke with my labors and went to sit in Nora's palace. She seemed content to let me wait, so I would be doing the same. As her assistant approached to give me the same answer as always, I changed things up.

"Actually, and I have no desire to offend, something personal has come up. Would it be possible to return in a few days instead?" I asked.

"Um . . ." the girl answered, clearly not expecting that request. "That should be fine, yes, though it will move you back to the end of the line again . . ."

"Oh that's all right," I said. "I'm not in any hurry at all." I grinned evilly and saw her blanch.

Good, good. Worry. I'd be giving her and Nora something to be concerned about soon enough.

CHAPTER 50

GRABBING ATTENTION

Five days in, and our construction was well under way. Chien and I were walking heavy equipment, so excavating a foundation had been easy as pie. Our turnout of concrete was also quite astounding, given the unbelievable amount of ash we'd started with. People were even bringing it to us themselves now and selling it wholesale for the pretty little stones I was making. Poor quality diamonds and other precious stones were flying off the shelves, and ash was replacing it at speed.

We got weird looks, of course, particularly as we ran through the process of turning ash into concrete—first into blocks, then in a big batch to bind the foundation together. It would be poor quality, but I didn't care; we weren't building structures with it, and I wasn't sticking around.

On the second day Isha revealed that she'd worked out a spell which made the stuff cure faster. I was dubious, but her magic was so different that it worked. In hours rather than days, the liquid stone hardened, seeming to take on full strength with little effort from her. Some days I really wanted to kiss her and, of course, I could and did just that. When we left, I would tell people that the concrete wouldn't last forever; I didn't want it disappointing or even harming someone, and I fully expected this construction to, much like another famous series of castles, sink into the swamp. However, I had no huge tracts of land upon which to build, nor any decent land. That was someone else's problem.

This morning, some people had come by to complain about us devaluing gems, and I just shrugged. Before I made my getaway, they might well be as valuable as the ash we wanted, and in fact, some of them were made from that too, just for funsies.

As I waved away the most recent irritated merchant, I returned to Chien.

"How are things progressing?" I asked.

"Isha's amazing," he answered.

"Oh, I know, but how are we doing?"

He grabbed the edges of his vest, which he'd gotten from someone in trade, and tutted. He looked exactly like a proper construction worker, minus the hard hat. I needed to get him a hard hat.

"So far ahead of schedule it's embarrassing. If we'd been doing this well in Atal, the whole city would have a wall thicker than you are tall. The interlinking blocks idea is working well too."

I'd suggested an almost Lego-like construction. Each block was molded to fit the one below it, then stacked slightly offset for added stability, one set upon another. We'd laid out a small tower already, something we'd be taking to two stories if we had to. Already it was as high as my shoulder.

"Excellent, then we continue onward." Magic really did bring a smile to my face.

Isha arrived shortly thereafter to have me come and sing the stone solid with her. I had no clue how it worked, but apparently having people sing with her helped, and watching her work was always weird. Her magic was so different from mine or Chien's. It was something I didn't get—magic that bent physics in ways I couldn't parse. That alone made the work more interesting to observe.

By sundown I was setting the entrance into place—beautiful arches for double doors, a smooth floor, and plenty of space. We'd been attracting attention as the days passed, and tomorrow morning I'd try to up my game even more.

Another three days passed, and in that time, we put in a second floor, still all stone, still building at a breakneck pace. I could only begin to imagine what would be possible with a properly trained crew of mages constructing buildings. In the future it might even be feasible for a few skilled magic users to throw up small towns in the span of days, with plumbing, windows, and pre-planned complex designs to make things easy.

The floors had to be made of wood, but that was easy enough to acquire. People were constantly gathering such things from the surrounding landscape, often accompanied by guards so as to avoid the enemy's troops. That said, it wasn't like it was a normal building material for houses here for some reason or another. It was probably the lack of more advanced woodworking techniques or metal connectors. To really get properly tight joints for buildings, metal tools and good measurement devices were a necessity.

I'd told Nora's people I'd see her in a few days, but for elves that was sort of an open-ended timeframe. Many of our older people were slow, very slow, in how they did their normal business—doing things when they got around to them. There was no hurry, no need to rush, at least most of the time. So, spending a week or two putting a small fortress on her front lawn wouldn't be seen as dragging my feet in coming to visit her at all.

However, the fact that I was putting a fortress on her front lawn would attract her attention and, I was hoping, spur her to stop being a bratty child and freaking see me already. Since a number of curious craftsmen were lining up to watch us finish our work, I'd given it good odds.

People had asked and been told they weren't getting the recipe for the concrete we were using. Sure, it was clear that there was ash, and water, and aggregate, but they didn't know the ratios, the method, or any other specifics. It'd be figured out eventually, but eventually was way down the line, and knowing that they had to first cook the ash and slake it wasn't something they'd likely stumble upon with ease. Others were interested in the way we were working the wood, and they'd likely have far more success. Metal tools would be much better, but if they paid attention, they'd be able to learn some of the basics of what we were doing with the softer material.

The roof was pretty rough, but as I finished and came back down to the ground, I was approached by a face I wasn't truly expecting.

"Excuse me, Justin," asked the same assistant who'd left me sitting bored in the waiting room for days and days.

"Ah, what a surprise to see you here. Is all well?" I asked innocently.

She gave me a slightly unamused look. "Elder Nora would like to see you promptly."

"How good to hear," I said with a smile.

She led me back up the hill to the complex the older elf had laid claim to, from which she now ruled this settlement. Rather than be taken to an empty room to be left alone, though, I was led deeper in. There were guards, who looked displeased, and plenty of aides as well, who also looked like I was a pain in their collective neck.

Nora's throne room was less ostentatious than the others I'd seen, smaller, almost homey. The room was some kind of stone, clearly smoothed with magic, and she naturally occupied a small chair on a wooden dais. However, there were tables all around, surrounded by elves deep in work. Nora, of course, was upon her little stone seat as I entered. She frowned as I was brought forward, tapping the arm of her seat. We spent some time looking at one another. Normally, she'd be the one to speak first, but she seemed content to glare at me. After about a minute of that I decided to speak. She could crush me if she wanted, but we both knew that she probably wouldn't.

"Atal and Cino are dead," I informed her.

CHAPTER 51

GETTING WHAT I WANTED

"Atal and Cino are dead," I repeated after a few minutes of staring at the elder before me as she sat silent.

"I know, and I heard you the first time. The people you came here with informed me on our journey."

I wanted to scream at her, to call her every name in the book for being a profound waste of my time. Honestly, though, it wasn't worth it. This woman, her people, her little power plays. I was leaving them at my first opportunity, and chewing her out wouldn't make that come any faster.

"Excellent," I said. "Well then, if there's nothing else."

"There is indeed something else," she snapped, finally.

"Please tell me what that is then," I answered flatly.

"You built a fortress at the edge of my city."

"I wanted your attention," I said simply. "Unsurprisingly, it succeeded."

There was a twitch developing in her eye. It was clear that too many people here were fawning over her, always happy she was around, happy when she fawned over them too. I was an outsider, though, someone who didn't care about her, or about her liking me. What would be the point in that, after all, since I was planning on leaving with haste?

"It did," she said. "You know, you could have shown some patience . . ." The look I gave her must have been capable of killing grass because she pulled back a bit. "Well, more patience. It isn't as if you were given a time limit for this mission of yours. I know well how they work."

"Just because others didn't demand my return does not mean I enjoy traipsing around the world like a vagrant. The list of things I would rather be doing than speaking with you, or some of the other old ones I've met for that matter, would stretch from your throne room to the docks. So, tell me, what did you want that you're delaying me further?"

"I could kill you, you know, for speaking to me like that," she hissed.

"You probably could, but then whatever it is you want would go unanswered."

"Personally, I was hoping that you would see reason, that you could be convinced to aid me in this war."

"No, I've had quite enough of war, and already provided your people quite enough aid. More and I would be too entangled in it for my liking."

"People are dying," she said. "Do you not care? Soldiers are going out every day, and not all come back. Surely you can see the destruction already present here, already done by our enemies. So many are gone because of what has happened, and many more may perish before it ends. With your abilities, though, the ones you showed with that fortress, with those new boats, we might be able to win faster, easier."

"Or you could negotiate, or surrender and end it. At worst, you and a handful of your closest advisors could flee, and I've told you where you might find somewhere new to call home. None would be able to oppose you if you moved into Cino's lands, and parts of Atal would be open as well. You've got the boats; you could leave tonight if you so desired." Technically, I knew of at least one ancient who really did want some of that tasty land, but screw this chick.

"And leave my people at that degenerate's hands!" she screamed, rising.

"I have met Uro's people, and perhaps he is worse than they are, but they did not seem inclined to pointless slaughter."

"They were killing people as I arrived," she said through gritted teeth.

"People who'd attacked them," I said. "I'm not here to defend their overall actions, but I will point out that they didn't want death."

"You are a very annoying man."

I didn't actually have anything to say to that, so I just shrugged. That particular gesture wasn't perfectly suited to my new world, but there were close enough equivalents that the point got across. It was clear that she had quite a lot more to say about that, but before she could, someone else entered in a clear flustered rush.

"Lady Nora," he began. "There's been an attack in the fields. We need aid."

"Please escort Justin here back to his building, and see to it that he stays there until I return," she said to one of her guards.

Now it was my turn to develop a twitch. Then again, if she didn't promptly return . . .

"I'll look forward to your return," I said. "Perhaps I'll think of some more fun things to do while I wait," I threatened.

The elder elf's lips formed a nearly perfect line before she waved me off. Several of her guards did indeed follow me along the way, taking a stance outside my makeshift home. They didn't try to enter, which was smart, but rather took places outside.

Hours passed, and I was bouncing around ideas of what I thought would be the biggest disturbance when I heard a small thud through an open window. Others followed in quick succession, each in turn. That was . . . odd, truly, greatly odd. I wasn't sure what exactly was going on, but I made a motion to my companions, for surely something was up.

We were preparing all around the building when a call came from the door. Knocking hadn't yet caught on, despite my best desires. Wooden doors just weren't all that common yet. Instead, a small voice came drifting up, asking to be allowed in.

After exchanging glances with Chien and Isha, I slowly, carefully opened my front door to find several figures standing in the evening darkness. There was a light mist around them, but even through that I could see the bodies of the guards on the ground.

"May we come in?" the leader asked from under a woven hat.

"I suppose," I replied, moving out of the way. They didn't seem aggressive, at least to us, and I had a good feeling about who these people represented.

The five who'd been outside slowly came into my structure, looking around. Their leader even went over to poke one of the walls while chuckling under his breath. That lasted only a few seconds before he took his hat off, and I saw the long strands of pure white. He was easily older than Nora and all smiles.

"Uro, I presume?" I asked.

"Yes, indeed, and if my spies tell me correctly, you're Justin. I hope you don't mind telling me what got you so worked up to do all of this." He smiled as he motioned to the walls and floors around us. "Because I'd really love to know."

CHAPTER 52

URO

I was flabbergasted. Most of the leaders of any size city I'd met on this journey were assholes, but this guy, this guy came to me. He'd heard that I was causing trouble to get his opponent to look at me, and he'd shown up on my doorstep.

"Well, this is a refreshing change. Atal and Cino are dead," I informed him.

"That's it? That's all of three seconds of information, and you built a fortress over it? Don't get me wrong, I'm grateful to know, as the loss of more of our eldest is a massive blow to our people as a whole, but this seems overdone."

"That's the boss," Chien said from the side before being shushed by Isha. It was clear that they thought I was the main actor here, and I didn't want too much attention diverted to either of them.

"It does seem like a bit much, doesn't it? But your enemy decided to make me wait for ages. Honestly, I'm ready to go home," I said, drawing his attention back to me.

He laughed heartily, seeming to understand.

"Understandable," he said. "Don't suppose I can convince you to tell me the method of construction for this?" he asked, still smiling.

"Would you be willing to help me and mine get out of this city and well off into the swamp?" I inquired.

Sure, I could have waited for Nora, but she seemed to have a stick so far up her behind, it was a wonder she could taste anything other than bark. Truly, I thought she might drag things out just to do so. Perhaps even trying to find excuses to keep me in the city like she'd done tonight, potentially for a long, long time. Having techniques she wanted would be enough for someone like that. Also, I liked this guy way more than her, so sharing this wouldn't be anything troublesome, for me.

"Just like that?" he asked, surprised at my small list of requirements.

"Just like that," I said. "She's already gotten some new items from me, so sharing this doesn't bother me in the least."

"Sure, we're leaving tonight," he said. "I can easily get your family out of here. Heh, I'll even send an escort with you for a bit."

"The second part isn't needed," I replied.

"Actually, I was hoping you could appraise them of the situation outside the swamps. If two ancients have died, there may be opportunities for my people, ones we didn't consider before."

Now it was my turn to laugh at him, and I did so. Uro was working his way up the list of my favorite older elves in a hurry.

"Something funny?"

"When I suggested exploring other options to Nora . . ." I had to stop.

"Oh, I see, didn't go well?"

"No."

"Well, I'd love to hear the details, but we do need to move."

"Certainly."

Isha and Chien looked at me, and with a nod we all knew that now was the time to go. Perhaps they'd had the same worries I did, perhaps not, but both trusted my judgement enough to follow when I was ready to make tracks.

For a moment something pinged in the back of my mind. Could this man be a fraud? Could he be an impersonator sent by Nora to milk me for secrets she didn't want to argue over? He was personable, and agreed with basically all of my points, as if he'd considered them, or been told them beforehand. Dye could change hair color, and as we left I could see that the guards were merely unconscious, not dead.

That doubt pinged louder as we gathered up the few possessions we cared about and began to make our way outside, and then I saw him cast. The movement of the magic was subtle, practiced, and powerful as he wove a spell around us I didn't quite understand. Words of power flowed like water from his mouth, and for the merest second I saw his aura pulse out, massive, yet so very well hidden, like a background noise you don't notice until someone else points it out.

Nobody but the highest ranked elders had magic like that. It was too strong, too big. He wasn't an ancient. He didn't have the terrible strength of Atal, or the might of Cino. He lacked the age of Rolan, or the practice of Matriarch Neera, but he was comparable to some I'd met, powerful in his own right.

Mist spread over the city, thick and deep like a blanket. There were cries of alarm, as surely Uro was known for this type of spell, but they were soon muffled, silenced by the billowing fog that moved outward like a wave, dimming the lights of fires, removing vision from all. Before the maker of the mists a window shone, bright and clear as day, allowing our group to move.

I could see my significant other trying to peek at what he was doing, watching how the spell formed and the simple magnitude of it. Did she know how this worked? Could she do it herself? Those were great questions for later, but I suspected that if she could, it would be of a much smaller magnitude than this, at least for the time being.

"Tell me of the construction while we move, Justin. I'm eager to hear of it, and I'm sure you're eager to be off." Uro walked as he spoke, leading our group forward to the docks. "Don't worry, the mist muffles sounds to a great extent."

I quickly rattled off the recipe, what he'd need, ratios, and a brief, but thorough step-by-step guide on what to do. Uro and his men nodded as I spoke, and didn't interrupt, attention as rapt as it could be while we moved through hostile territory. It wouldn't matter if they didn't pay attention, though. With our memories, they could easily replay these moments and hear it all again.

Once I'd finished, Chien chimed in with a few quick tips and tricks. I may have been the one who came up with a lot of the ideas, but when it came to practical experience, he was excelling beyond my means. Once I introduced something, I tried to be done with it, letting others work out how to use it, both because I didn't know and I knew they'd come up with things different than I could imagine; it also didn't hurt that I had so very many projects going. Chien, however, did quite a bit of work with things like concrete—personal experience that I hadn't grown myself.

"You give away so much for so little," he said when I finished.

"It's not exactly a secret," I said. "The basic formula is known in the city of Atal."

"Oh, I see," he said with a small giggle. "So the price is really nothing to you."

"Nothing to me, but much to you, I'd wager."

"Yes, indeed."

As we moved, I wondered how Nora had fought against this kind of spell. It seemed so powerful. With the ability to move your people unhindered through contested ground, you could be anywhere, everywhere, and there'd be little to do about it.

We reached the boats without a problem and began throwing things in before I got my answer. My body locked up, freezing joints and limbs that wouldn't respond. I saw Uro and his men tense, then with a pulse of their auras, they were able to move again, sluggishly, weakly, but they could move.

"She's here," one of them said as I tried, and failed, to do as they had. My own aura just wasn't strong enough, and I'd not practiced their technique. Uro's spell began to falter, thinning, not to nothing, but greatly, while figures appeared in the nearby gloom, parting their way forward.

"I certainly am," a familiar, cold, feminine voice answered.

CHAPTER 53

MISTAKES

After she spoke, a bolt flew from the gloom, striking Uro in the chest. Icy blue shone over his body as he froze, unmoving, unable to respond to the actions of the elves quickly heading toward us out of the mists.

Behind me, I heard Isha draw in a breath, only to stop and begin coughing. Footsteps all around faltered and ceased as one after another, the group came to a halt. It was no mystery to me either, for as she approached, Nora seemed to be exuding some form of paralysis, keeping us still and in place. The elders with Uro resisted for a few moments, but even to them it was pointless, being rendered immobile and at the mercy of our captor.

"What's all this then?" Nora asked as she approached, looking us over. "Looks like we finally caught up with you, Uro."

"Should we dispose of them ma'am?" one of her soldiers asked.

"No, I'll deal with this one personally; the others, we'll hold. Perhaps they can be brought back to their senses when this is all over. Search them thoroughly though."

"Understood." I couldn't see the man behind me, as he began to rifle through someone's things. As he did so, the older elf turned to me, pulling her head to the side.

I considered casting but struggled with the idea. Songs and movement weren't needed for my magic, though they did work sort of like a crutch—movements that felt right for the magic helping to focus. Regardless, she'd have defenses, and if they noticed me building anything big, I had no doubts about what they'd do.

Normal spells wouldn't work; that was clear. What about something like I'd used on the soldiers in the cave, something pernicious and quiet? Maybe, but I didn't have the time I had then, and there were too many people nearby. Gasses like that might affect my allies if I wasn't careful.

"What do we have here? Justin, I'm surprised to find you in this situation. You know, had you only waited for me, you'd have been able to walk out of here freely so very soon. Were you with him the whole time? That would be a surprise, wouldn't it. We'll have to find out together what the truth is."

She was teasing me, dangling the same damn carrot she'd been playing with during the entirety of my stay. Man, I hated this woman, her games, her stupid words. She'd wanted to trap me here, and now she had me. While I silently seethed, trying to think of something, anything I could do to stop her, hands began to go through my pouches and clothes.

Nora had turned, taking a few steps away and moving toward Uro. With a wave he could speak again.

"We don't have to fight anymore," he pled. "The messenger. One of us can leave, a new land, no competition. Consider it, Nora—an end to this madness." His words were jerky, probably some interference designed to keep him from singing, and breathless too, so no shouts.

"Another ploy, at this point, really? As if I'd believe that." Uro tried to speak again, but his words froze, almost into a choking sound.

"We have something," the guard examining me interrupted before she could finish whatever she was doing.

"What?"

"These are . . . weird," he said, bringing over a pouch he'd pulled out, looking confused.

"Hmm?" Nora said, dumping the pouch out into her palm. "Are these . . . Wherever did you get this? And what have you suspended them in? Are these from that old monster up north?" As she spoke she looked at me, blinking.

She looked, and I looked too. She'd dumped the crystals into her hand. How long I'd had those, bouncing around in my things. Of all the things I'd considered doing with them, now there was a chance, now I could do something, defend myself.

"You're just a bundle of secrets, aren't you, Justin?" Nora continued. "I'll need to have all of them, of course, and I will. Perhaps your little assistant would be willing to serve as *motivation*, or . . . Yes, I think the woman would be better, wouldn't she?"

The tyrant smiled as she looked at Isha, and I saw crimson. How could these people follow her? Did they not realize what she was like? Didn't matter, though, did it? She'd made her decision, so I made mine.

How little she understood about what she held. How little she knew. I didn't doubt she'd seen similar crystals before; with her age and power, that was a given. Had she seen any made by one of us, though? No, if she had, she'd have thrown those as far from herself as she could. Instead, the greedy elder clasped them in her hand.

Those were mine, though. They were my mana in crystal form. They obeyed me, and so I commanded them, reaching out with my mind to the power I'd put into the small grains, suspended in their artificial diamond prisons. It was a command I was so fond of, one I'd used so many times before, one she deserved.

BURN

In an instant, each of the little grains ignited with the force of a wildfire. Her magic fought against them, but it didn't matter, didn't change the fact that she was holding that much energy that went from solid to heat in an instant. To make those, I'd had to focus mountains of power into such a small space, mountains that now burst like a ruptured dam, pouring back out into the world in a torrent of flame.

There wasn't a shockwave. That was the only thing that surprised me. No, one moment her fist closed around the set of little jewels, and the next it was an inferno. The scent of charred flesh filled the air as the fire grew brighter and brighter, consuming her hand and then her lower arm. She didn't even have time to scream as it melted flesh and carbonized bone.

As the fire took her arm, I was the only one prepared. Others looked on in horror as their leader suffered and stumbled as her spell failed. Whatever she'd been doing must have taken active involvement that she was no longer capable of, because as she burned, we were free.

We were free, and I was ready.

CHAPTER 54

DOCKSIDE BATTLE

The first to go was the guard who'd searched me. He was clearly an enemy and standing right before me—unfortunate for him because I wasn't in a particularly merciful mood.

I placed my hand on the back on the stunned man's head and simply released a wave of kinetic energy. There was a *pomf* sound and a spray of red gore. Nobody could take that sort of an attack at point blank range without some defense, and his had been sorely lacking.

For a beat, nobody responded, and then chaos reigned. Unsurprisingly, Uro was the first to engage. From beside me I heard his voice raise, and instantly a tingle crossed my skin as he did . . . something. I wasn't entirely sure what, but it was followed by screaming, so I guessed it'd proven effective. Others weren't far behind him, though, as shouts and screams rang out all around me.

As my second target fell, spewing a fountain of blood all over the ground, I spun a quick shield around myself, and just in time. A significant force slammed into my side, tossing me and my bubble into the wall of a nearby mud building.

"You bastard!" came the shouting voice of one of the others, presumably some physical type magic user, since he'd tackled me a good ten feet and nearly shattered a mud brick wall. "I'll kill you! I'll rip off your head!"

"Shh, stop yelling," I answered quietly as I sent a wave of yellow smoke at him with a motion. Summoning this wasn't something I'd practiced, but it came easier than I'd imagined it would.

"Stop yelling? You insan—" He was cut off by his own coughing as the chlorine reached his lungs, drawing more in. "Wha . . ." The coughing continued, and I kept pouring the poison into his face.

"You really should've listened," I chided as I looked up and back toward the others.

To my endless relief, Chien had moved beside Isha and was projecting the thickest bubble I imagined he could. Perhaps that wouldn't have been enough against a dedicated assault by some of those involved in this battle, but they were getting only stray shots as Isha grabbed Chien and began to run for cover. In the few moments I had, I noticed her scream at one of the other guards who got a little too close, sending the man reeling backward.

Satisfied that my loved ones were fleeing as they should, I turned back to the others. Uro's men were surrounded, and slightly outnumbered, but there was hope for them yet. Nora's people had been deprived of their strongest fighter. He was currently locked in combat with three of the guards and looked to be winning.

There was a wave of auras over the battlefield, and I began searching them. Nora was down, but not dead, it appeared. She was writhing on the ground, skin and flesh stitching itself back together as I watched on. It was like some kind of CGI effect. That wouldn't do at all.

It was truly surprising that the sizable bolt of kinetic energy I sent screaming at the injured healer shattered upon her skin. With great interest, I watched as the spell fizzled out against her. Was this more of the resistance I'd seen earlier? Still not knowing how that worked, I was a bit put out. After all, my best attacks were magical in nature.

Another of the guards saw me shooting at their leader and apparently took exception to that. He ignored the man coughing up what was left of his lungs at my feet and sent a storm of missiles my way, only for them to bounce harmlessly off my shield. I'd worked long and hard on my kinetic magic, so it was stronger than most, but it was still a threat. My responding volley proved more effective, but there was still some resistance, leaving large marks covering his body.

That was frustrating. I really needed to get to the bottom of their resistances. I watched closely as another of my attacks hit him, trying to focus on what he was doing. I observed that the spell unwound as it neared his skin, dissolving against what looked like his aura. Another quick look confirmed that all of the combatants, save myself and mine, were pulsing theirs out. Did that have something to do with it? With a sigh, I realized that now really wasn't the time.

While I was spacing out, my opponent pulled together another spell, slamming me and my shield back into the wall once more. It cracked, and bricks began to fall off of it, opening a sizable hole in the structure. On a lark, I grabbed one of those chunks with my magic, accelerating it toward my attacker as fast as I could. Atal had been thrilled to have a weapon that could do something similar, and I assumed he'd known about whatever they were doing.

Surprisingly, that worked. Most of my attacks had been stronger than that, but its effect was an order of magnitude more. The piece of mud masonry impacted the caster in the stomach, and he crumbled, tossed back by the energy imparted in it.

"Huh, guess it only affects magic," I said, hardly even thinking about it. "Now, where were we?"

Nora was trying to rise, one arm a char-covered stump, but she still looked out of sorts as she tried to point a hand to where Uro and the others were fighting. It'd already been decided that I would tolerate no more of her, so I needed to do something about that.

We were close enough to the docks that I could see them, so I simply wrapped magic around one of the rafts. Straining to my limit, I pulled upon my strength, images of a rope wrapping around it, and yanked as hard as I could. Slowly at first, but rapidly gaining speed, it rose and began flying at Nora.

The fighting seemed to pause as I worked, falling away into the background. For seconds that stretched on like minutes, the world slowed to a crawl. I could see the moment Nora turned, looking at the approaching calamity, the widening of her eyes, then everything sped back up.

There was a brief scream, the barest starts of a truly terrified shriek, before it was cut off by the crashing of wood into flesh. Not willing to risk her surviving, I sent a blast of flames into the shattered remnants of the vessel. Perhaps she couldn't be burned so easily, but wood was well known for doing so.

"Enough!" came a reverberating boom from Uro.

I had to cover my ears as the elder elf began to speak, amplifying his voice enough that the ground seemed to shake.

"This has gone on long enough. Cease at once. Take your injured and go back to your homes. Your leader is dead. This fight is over. Now cease."

Picking myself up off the ground, I cast a glance into the home I'd been slammed into. There was a woman, hair disheveled and cheeks streaked with tears, holding a child, the young girl looking much the same as her mother. Both trembled, weeping and curled up in the far corner of the room.

"Please . . ." the mother begged as she saw me looking in at her. "Please don't hurt us."

"Don't worry, I . . ." Then I realized what this must look like. I'd slammed through their wall, hurling pieces of their home at people and sending spells, decidedly designed to kill, all around, the whole time quietly talking to myself.

From her perspective I must be a terror, a villain in the night, ruining her home and an immediate threat to her and her child. That bothered me in a visceral way. Deep in my chest it hurt to know that to this woman, to these innocent people, I must be a horror born of nightmares.

By the time I realized I still needed to keep my guard up and turned, it looked like the fighting had stopped. Several of those still standing were surrounding Uro protectively, while others had taken their comrades in arms and were carrying them away quickly. Uro looked pensively at the pyre his former enemy lay beneath, eyes almost regretful.

CHAPTER 55

AWAY AGAIN

Though they seemed nervous about it, Uro's guards allowed me to approach as he looked upon his enemy's pyre.

"I would have preferred she lived through this," he said sadly.

"Do not regret the fate she brought upon herself, Uro; you gave her a chance. Perhaps you think she'd have changed, but even with my short experience with her, I doubt that."

"Perhaps, perhaps not, but now there is no chance for change. Now my people as a whole are weaker than they could have been, and now more will suffer than need to."

It was clear to me that he was the one who should be leading regardless. Perhaps he understood that this war had few possible endings, but still he wanted to do what was best for everyone, not just himself. He'd been willing to consider options, to quit the field, if only to spare others pain. Perhaps that was an issue with him, but it also showed where his interests lay: not with self-aggrandizement, but with the care of his people. Ultimately, he'd make a better future for them.

While I contemplated this beside him, I saw Chien and Isha begin to make their way from whatever cover they'd found, peeking out at first, then coming toward us slowly, looking for threats.

"Uro, it would probably be best for everyone if we avoided further conflict here today. What's left of Nora's people are likely to be coming soon, and they'll fight if they see you here."

"A wise observation," he said. "Let us go for now. Come daylight I'll take the necessary steps to finally end this conflict." He looked at me from the corner of his eye. "Are you still satisfied to leave now? Some might say I owe you something for the service you've done me today."

I considered for a few moments. I really didn't want anything for myself other than what I'd wanted before.

"All I truly desire is to leave peacefully, Uro, but there is something else you can do for me."

"What's that?" he asked cautiously, eyes stern.

"During the battle I damaged a home here. Would you see to it that those whose homes I wrecked are either given the one I built or another of good standing? The same for whoever owned that boat?" I pointed to the place where I'd seen the mother and her child, the massive yawning hole in their home clearly evident.

Uro's lips formed the smallest of smiles. "You have my word they'll be taken care of."

I nodded to him. His word was good enough for me. Could he betray his word and give those whose homes and livelihoods I'd damaged nothing? Sure, but that didn't seem like the kind of person he was. If I had to guess, I'd say that when he came back they'd be quickly aided. After all, it was clear to see that he cared about people as a whole. Sounds began to drift to us from farther in the city, indicating that people were coming our way, so we quickly got moving. Getting to my boat was easy enough, and Uro's men rushed to their own. Before anybody made it to us, we were well underway, sailing out to the lake.

The guards near the harbor must have been involved in the battle because nobody tried to stop us as we set sail. Our craft cut through the water, driven by magic, into the large central lake, pushing away from the city.

As we fled, I looked back. A number of people had gathered upon the shore. Most were surrounding the flaming wreckage, looking on in shock at what had become of their leader. None of them tried to put it out, seeming to know that there was nothing they could do. One, however, looked on after us.

Curz had been the one to bring us to this place. We'd been lost, looking for aid, and he'd helped us find this settlement. Sure, I wasn't happy about his deception with Uro's men, but we'd understood each other to an extent. Now he watched on as we left, eyes sad, tears streaking down his cheeks.

Would this be my destiny? To forever be forced from my home, to forever leave destruction in my wake? Even when I tried to do good, things broke. My childhood village had burned before they spurned me. The city I'd settled into had been broken and decimated by war. Now, behind me, another place was left in pain, with more suffering.

No, I refused to accept that. I'd always done what I could to protect, to save people where and when I was able. I'd brought not only pain but also advancement, hope for the future. Perhaps there would be suffering at times. That was life; but I could also bring good to this world.

Beside us, one of Uro's canoes pulled up, a pair of soldiers inside it. "Uro asked us to show you the fastest route northward, if you want the help."

"We'd be grateful," I told them, and they pulled forward, picking up a good amount of speed.

His soldiers didn't speak to us as we cut through the night. Odd, because I knew he'd originally wanted more info on the boats and the like, but perhaps he was reconsidering. An image of betrayal sparked in my mind, but I quickly extinguished it. If Uro had wanted us dead, he'd had the chance earlier. It's likely he just wanted us gone.

"You seem contemplative," Isha said as she joined me where I sat on the boat.

"It's been a long night," I told her.

She leaned in and kissed my cheek, soft lips cool against my skin, and settled beside me, her scent wafting my way. Soap wasn't really a big thing in this world, but people still washed. It made for an altogether different smell than I was used to on Earth—more wild, tinged with the smoke from the fires everyone kept, and sweat that seemed to be everywhere. This mixed with herbs and flowers that some women, even my Isha, sometimes used to scrub themselves, both to improve their scent and to ward off insects. All this was added to the smell of the branches we often slept upon, to form its own perfume.

"Things will get better," she assured me.

"How do you know? How do you trust that?"

"Because I trust you."

I had to hold back tears, wondering what I'd done in either of my lives to deserve someone like her.

CHAPTER 56

OFF AND AWAY

We didn't stop, not at all. Our boat moved through the water at speed day and night; while I rested, Chien drove it, while he slept, I did. Isha might not have been too good at propelling us, but she still pulled her weight. We didn't want for tasty snacks or a properly set up sleeping area. Her skills might not excel in combat, but when it came to supply, she beat me soundly.

"Do you think they'll be okay?" Isha asked me as I lay down to rest three days in.

"Probably," I answered. "With only one leader left, most people should fall in line now."

"And those that don't?"

I frowned, unsure what exactly would be the right answer. There were a few options, a few ways things could go, but honestly I didn't really care. That in mind, I decided to go with the truth.

"Might be bad for them. If they're smart, they might leave. Or they might fight, but honestly, I hope they manage to find some peace, regardless. We should leave it, though. It's not our business unless they decide to come and make it our business."

"Hmm, people do like to stay near where they were born," she said thoughtfully.

Thinking back on it, I realized she was right. Even now, I hated being away from Atal. I hated it with every fiber of my being. That was odd, wasn't it? Back on Earth I hadn't had such worries or concerns. It had seemed normal to me to go off to college; moving wasn't that big a deal, but it was here.

Chien and Isha weren't as vocal, but I had a feeling they didn't love it either. There were hardly any merchants, even fewer that went between regions. Each little country or city-state was independent, unwilling to spread. Even those elves that had been stuck in the far north hesitated to run south when a spot opened up they could easily take.

"What's that look?" Isha asked.

"We hate moving around," I muttered. "That's bad."

She quirked an eyebrow at me. "Why?"

"My inventions aren't going to spread at any real rate, nor will new things come back to me."

"How horrible," she said. "You'll just have to do more inventing yourself."

"No, we need people to trade with," I said, "to go out and think of new ways of doing things, and to bring those new ways between cities."

"Justin, you're hardly making any sense. Why would we need that?"

"Imagine if no traders ever came to a village," I said.

"Okay, that would be unfortunate, but it's not like they're really needed."

From her perspective, she was right. A village could live without others coming and going, frequently or infrequently. The village where we were born didn't get them often, after all, at least not before I began working copper. Most of them could make the basics themselves.

"But copper will never spread, nor steel, nor new ways to do magic." As I spoke she shrugged. "We need to do something about that."

With a frown she closed in on me, her face right next to mine. "You made a promise to me," she growled. "We're not going off on another fool trip for some time."

I nearly laughed at her reaction but checked myself quickly. If there was anything I'd learned about women over the years, it was that not taking them seriously was a recipe for disaster, that and telling them to calm down.

"No, love, we're not, but I need to keep it in mind. Maybe set things up for other people to do it."

Isha gave a jerking nod. "Good, just regulate those ideas of yours."

Regardless of what I told her, the thought concerned me. I needed to know if this was something ingrained in our race or merely a function of the fact that we aged strangely and in so doing, became sedentary by the time we were strong enough to move about. Because it was a fact that the transfer of information built societies, and I certainly had a society to build.

"So," I said, trying to change the subject to one she'd prefer. "Been thinking of names?"

Isha blushed. "Well, a bit. If a boy, after my father; if a girl, after your mother. How does that sound?" she asked as she cuddled up next to me, nibbling at my ear.

"Works for me," I replied as I kissed her.

"I swear," Chien added from the front of the craft, "if you two start fucking while I'm trying to steer, I will stop this boat. It's one thing if you're in private, but quite another when you're out in the open."

We both had a good laugh at that, but he seemed serious. Perhaps the fact that we'd been separated from the populace in our last city had irked him.

"We need to find you a girl for yourself," Isha said.

"I'm quite good just borrowing them, thanks. Whatever would you do if I came home all silly in the head because some girl had caught me like a bird in a snare?"

"Laugh?" I suggested.

"Exactly, not really the most useful thing for us to be doing, now is it? At least one of us needs to keep his head on straight."

"And you're the voice of reason now?" Isha teased.

"Darling Isha, I've always been the voice of reason. Now sometimes that reason will laugh at you, and sometimes it likes to chase skirts, just to relax. That's just for fun, though, not for anything more."

"Chien, if you give some girl a child and abandon her . . ." Isha began to threaten.

"Then I'll be just like my father, but don't worry. If I find out I've fathered a child, I'll make sure they don't starve or suffer."

That response hardly inspired confidence in me, but it was something. No family courts here, no child support, or anything like that. Honestly, I wasn't even aware of anyone around who could trace family lines, though that should be possible with magic, if I was understanding the bio-magic people like my mother had.

"If you do, let me know," I said. "I'll be happy to make sure the kid gets a proper education."

At that, our current skipper looked back and nodded slightly, looking thoughtful.

EPILOGUE

Rolan

I looked out over the forest with concern, hand tapping the railing I'd grown years ago, letting my eyes scan the horizon.

"Something bothers you, Ancient?" asked one of my advisors.

She was one of the more useful ones—young, skilled, and good at reading my moods. The last bit was something that was becoming rarer by the day. With my many years of experience dulling my facial expressions to almost nothing unless I was trying. This woman, though, not even in her hundredth year, could tell when I was bothered.

"Yes, what do you make of the reports we received yesterday from the borderlands?" I asked, seeing how well she understood other things—educating was part of my duty.

"The monsters coming from the west? None of them were particularly dangerous, even if there's been an increase." Ah, a failure to see the bigger picture then.

"Not the numbers, but the type."

"Um . . . yes, I think the messenger said they were more of the kind that frequented the plains, among the rarer ones we'd see."

That the scout had known they were plains monsters was surprising. That he knew they were uncommon to see in the plains bordering our lands more so. We'd need to see where he'd picked that up and expand the training to others if we could.

"They're not rarer, merely not commonly seen in this area. Those beasts frequent the far side of the plains to the western border. More than that, tell me about them."

"Birds . . . a few deer-like creatures." Her mind worked, eyes focusing as she thought back. "Everything that was described was . . . fast? Fast and weak?"

"Indeed, the first wave, the first ones to get to us if something were to cause them to flee. The most likely to flee as well."

"Flee what, Ancient?" she inquired.

"Sadly, I don't know everything, child. The beasts are more sensitive than we are, though. If they're fleeing, it is because they feel they must, that there is some danger. Send a unit of scouts into the central lands to see what they can learn."

"As you command."

Briefly, I graced her with a true smile before turning back to the woods. This sign of trouble was slight, so slight, but it had meaning; all such things had meaning. Something was going wrong, perhaps today, or tomorrow, or a decade, or century from now, but it was going wrong. We'd need to find out what it was so it could be addressed properly.

Matriarch Neera

The glacier was a hive of activity, not frantic, not worried, but all moving. A chance, a brief chance for me and my people to leave this place and take new, better lands had appeared, and I wasn't going to waste it. Moving so many took preparation, though, preparation that we couldn't do overnight. No, it would take work, arduous work over some time, but doable.

"All well, Matriarch?" came the question from beside me.

"Hmm? Oh yes, thinking that I might need to thank that boy somehow."

The man laughed. He was one of the few who got my jokes and one of the even fewer I'd had as lovers over the years. Some liked to flit from man to man, but I found it didn't appeal to me, and worse, if and when one of them died, I always spent years mourning.

"The leader or the one who impregnated that girl?" he chuckled.

"Both? Yes, both. They both did us a service in the end. How is she?" The girl may have traded herself away for a trinket, but that didn't mean we should ignore her. After all, her child would be powerful if it took after the father at all.

"She's well, as are all the others. Those three really did change people, didn't they?"

He was right. For the first time in a long time we were doing more than just holding and growing. All those with the power in their veins had seen what those travelers could do, and all of them wanted more now. In the past this would have been a problem, a disaster as they died against the ice, but now? Now it was an opportunity. We could teach them and use them to take the land I wanted.

"For the better, love. The extra stones for heating will be invaluable too."

"True, but I would have preferred if they'd not stirred the shrikes from their nests." His comment made me frown, for I knew that to be so as well.

"Yes, are they getting closer to us?"

"Thankfully, no, at least not since I heard last."

The ice shrikes were a potent problem, but one I seldom had to deal with. They lived in their crevice, slowly chipping away as it closed in on them, slowly living out their lives and bothering none. That was unless someone took it upon themselves to stir the flock up. Then they would rage. Such beasts were also an irritant to deal with, the survivors coming out as more and more potent monstrosities until they could be fully destroyed.

"That one might be our fault, though, as none of us thought to warn him." I knew he'd survived. I'd heard reports from the rare messenger from the western coast. At least there had been no incredible chaos. However, I would need to keep a lookout for that boy in the future, see what became of him, if anything.

Uro

The man was led before me and pushed to his knees.

"Will you swear your loyalty or accept exile?" I asked. It was the same question I'd asked so many others.

"Damn you! Murderer, destroyer! You didn't even manage to kill her yourself, you coward!"

"I'll accept that as a no."

His head was pushed down as the executioner approached, bringing down his turtle-shell blade in a blurred arc. The man, Curz by name, had been one of the last holdouts. Now his head fell from his body, blood soaking the stones of the central square, a spurt covering my feet as I nodded to the soldiers who held the others that had resisted.

Curz would never have sworn, and I'd seriously doubted he'd actually accept exile, even if he said he would. I think he knew that his fate had been sealed, and chosen instead to rail against me rather than ask for mercy. Of course, that suited me fine, as I had a perfect example for what would happen to the rest of his little group.

Next, however, a shaking boy was brought before me. And a boy he was, hardly an adult, perhaps not even old enough to hold accountable. He too, however, had tried to fight, but now, with tears streaming from his eyes, there was no fight left in him. Another perfect example for those coming next.

The young man was forced to his knees in the blood of the one who'd led him here, his whole body trembling like a wilted leaf in the wind. I saw his eyes flick to the blade, to the body, to the ground around him.

"Will you swear loyalty or accept exile?" I asked again.

"I . . . May I stay if I swear? This is my home," he begged.

"You may, though you will owe me labor for the trouble you've caused." That was the deal for all of them—a term of work for those who hadn't surrendered when I'd told them to. Nothing extreme, but enough to rebuild some of the damage our cities had taken.

"I swear loyalty to you, Uro," he replied woodenly.

Another motion, and he was taken away to be processed, told where and when to go and sent home. He'd be watched, and he'd never be trusted, but he could live in peace. Of course, if he went back upon his word, there would be no further mercy. This was his one and only chance.

Others followed, all but one taking the example of the boy and either surrendering to my rule or accepting their exile with grace. I certainly hoped none required me to deal with them later, but that would be their choice, not mine. I retreated to look over the city. Like the others, it was rebuilding and fast, and if early reports were to be believed, better than ever. That Justin had brought me a potent new tool for that purpose, and my people were exploiting it for all it was worth. Walls would be bigger and stronger, the foundations for homes set without the need to haul nearly as much stone or wood from outside, instead using more local ingredients. It would pay dividends in the future, and I didn't even have to keep dealing with the creator of that material.

His requests had been simple, to leave peacefully and give a proper home to the family whose house he'd ruined. The latter showed a good sense of justice, a desire to do good that I could fully get behind. I also didn't hesitate. Refusing such a minor thing, and in the process potentially angering such a fierce foe, was a fool's errand. One my former enemy allowed her pride to blind her to.

Those days were behind us. Now was the time to fix things— mend broken walls and broken bonds of kinship. It would take many years, but eventually we'd be restored to what we once were, or perhaps even better.

ABOUT THE AUTHOR

Wandering Agent is the North Carolina–based author of the Melody of Mana series as well as other fantasy and isekai stories.

JOIN THE FELLOWSHIP

follow us on our socials

 podiumentertainment.com

 @podiumentertainment

 /podiumentertainment

 @podium_ent

 @podiumentertainment